Sins & Lies

BOOK 2 OF ENZO'S TRILOGY

THE SINS SERIES

LEXXI JAMES

Contents

Get Your Freebies! — vii
Please Note... — ix

1. Enzo — 1
2. Kennedy — 7
3. Enzo — 14
4. Kennedy — 21
5. Enzo — 30
6. Enzo — 38
7. Enzo — 48
8. Enzo — 60
9. Enzo — 71
10. Kennedy — 77
11. Kennedy — 83
12. Kennedy — 88
13. Kennedy — 98
14. Enzo — 103
15. Enzo — 107
16. Kennedy — 114
17. Enzo — 123
18. Kennedy — 129
19. Kennedy — 137
20. Enzo — 145
21. Enzo — 150
22. Enzo — 157
23. Kennedy — 162
24. Enzo — 170
25. Kennedy — 176
    Epilogue | Enzo — 181

SINS OF THE SYNDICATE

1. Ivy	187
2. Ivy	195
3. Ivy	199

MARKED

1. Jess	209
2. Jess	212
3. Mark	229
About the Author	235

SINS & Lies
Book 2 in Enzo's Trilogy
The SINS Series
Copyright © 2024 Lexxi James

www.LexxiJames.com
All rights reserved. Lexxi James, LLC.
Independently Published

With Grateful Appreciation to My Remarkable Editing Team
KE
Jamie Ryter, The Ryter's Proof Editing
With Special Thanks to the Lexxi James VIP Beta Readers

Cover by Book Sprite, LLC
Image by Wander Aguiar
Wander Aguiar Photography LLC
Models Stephen & Dina @ ZINK MODEL

No part of this publication may be reproduced, distributed, or transmitted in any form or by any means, including photocopying, recording, or other electronic or mechanical methods, without the prior written permission of Lexxi James, LLC. Under certain circumstances, a brief quote in reviews and for non-commercial use may be permitted as specified in copyright law. Permission may be granted through a written request to the publisher at LexxiJamesBooks@gmail.com.

This is a work of fiction. Names, characters, places, and incidents are the product of the author's imagination. Specific named locations, public names, and other specified elements are used for impact, but this novel's story and characters are 100 percent fictitious. Certain long-standing institutions, agencies, and public offices are mentioned, but the characters involved are wholly imaginary. Resemblance to individuals, living or dead, or to events which have occurred is purely coincidental. And if your life happens to bear a strong resemblance to my imaginings, then well done and cheers to you! You're a freaking rock star!

Get Your Freebies!

Join Lexxi's VIP Reader list and be the first to know about new releases, free books, special prices, and giveaways!

www.LexxiJames.com/freebies

The **SINS** Series in order:

SINS of the Syndicate
SINS & Ivy
SINS: The Debt

SINS: The Deal
>> SINS & Lies
SINS & Temptation

Please Note...

This is book two of a trilogy and will end in a cliffhanger.

If you are a fan of my work, please be warned:
This trilogy is dark. It is darker than the first three books in the *SINS of the Syndicate* series and is my darkest romance to date.

On the morally gray scale, Enzo D'Angelo veers to black. His adversaries have no morals. Bodily harm and graphic violence will be described.

Like haunted houses and carnival rides, only you know your limits. Your mental health matters.

Welcome back to Enzo's world.

CHAPTER 1
Enzo

THERE ARE two types of people in the world: those who tiptoe slowly into the shallow end of madness, and those who prefer to dive in head-first and drown in their darkness.

I am the latter.

I am Enzo. And, for the most part, I'm devoid of the petty inconveniences of feelings or emotions. Or for that matter, a conscience.

Normally, I carry out my wrath with surgical precision, strategic in who dies and who loses limbs.

Today, I'm out for blood.

Someone took my *Bella*, though I doubt if you asked her she'd say she was mine. Knowing her, she'd give you some bullshit about how she's her own woman and that no one owns her.

Sweet little Kennedy. How wrong you are.

And I don't give a shit if she was kidnapped. She'll pay for every goddamned minute of the torture she's putting me through right now, plotting vengeance on whoever took her.

Which, by all accounts, is probably my uncle.

The only sibling of my father, Andretti D'Angelo grew up in my father's shadow. Both were smart, wealthy, and lethal. But where my father was tall and dark, Uncle Andre was stodgy and pale.

Unlike my father, whose demonic side could sometimes be tempered, Uncle Andre never switched it off. It's no surprise he's the prime suspect in my father's disappearance.

As well as the reason my brothers and I continuously draw straws for who gets to rip out his toenails.

So, for the record, I despise my uncle. And I hate him that much more when he plays with my toys.

"Can you at least wait for me to get there?" Dante barks through the phone. "Just think this through."

I'd say yes if his thirst for blood would kick in. But my brother's tone reeks of rational thought and protectiveness.

Who has time for that shit?

My eyes drift to the arsenal sprawled across the seat beside me. Two Glocks, three hunting knives, an AK-47, and a dozen hand grenades. "Rest assured, Dante. I have thought this through."

Though now that I'm thinking it over, I blow out a breath and sigh. This is my uncle. We own half the criminal underworld. He owns the other half.

Damn, I should've brought the Uzi.

"Let's discuss this," he offers. He may as well have offered me a subscription for anal waxing.

My voice is so calm I barely recognize it. "Go back to hosting your little tea party, Dante." Aka, my birthday. "I've got this."

"You've got a raging hard-on for some girl, that's what you've got. And that girl's about to get you killed."

He's right about one thing: my hard-on. But getting killed has never been in the cards for me, and when it comes to her being *some* girl, he's dead wrong.

No woman has bear-trapped my attention the way my *Bella* has.

Which nudges my foot to floor the gas. I know all the ways my uncle might be touching her. Hurting her. Sharing her.

And I know the million and one ways I'll retaliate if he does.

"Enzo, it's a really bad time for you to declare war with Uncle Andre. Or have the feds breathing down our backs. Both of which will happen if you rush in, reckless and gun blazing and led by your dick," Dante warns, frustrated.

"I'm not led by my dick," I lie.

Ugh. I'm so totally led by my dick. But what does he expect? He's been starved for months, and Kennedy's cunt tastes like heaven. "You saw the footage," I remind him.

"I saw a black BMW 4-series. Lots of people drive them. And?" he asks.

"And?" My jaw clenches hard. I can't believe I have to connect the dots for him. "Uncle Andre and his band of dickless thugs all drive them. Because the cheap bastard won't spring for the 8-series." I scoff. "He snatched her, Dante. Right from under our noses in your own goddamned club."

"It might've been one of his men."

"Him. His men. Whoever it was is about to learn that no one steals from me."

"So now this is a cautionary tale about stealing?"

"It's about war. Thermonuclear fucking war."

My heart thuds loudly in my ears. Is it one man? More than one? Are they forcing themselves on her? Taking turns with her body as she screams? Or all at once...

"Enzo?" His voice is like a pesky gnat in my ear now, barely registering over the roar of my own rage. "Listen to me. Wait for us!"

"If I need you, I'll call." With a quick flick of my finger, I end the call. My focus lasers in on just one thing: getting Kennedy Luciano back.

The road narrows tight against a thick band of trees. So much so that my foot eases up on the gas.

Hundreds of secluded acres, a maze of dense woods and ravines. As a child, these woods were my schoolyard. My wonderland. When my father and Uncle Andre were at least on speaking terms.

I think back, fondly recalling the mangled remains of a man, eyes bulged and neck broken. The sharp bone of his shin protruded through his flesh. His left hand gnawed away.

Uncle Andre dismissed it as just some hiker bad on his luck. Quite the coincidence, considering that the trident tattoo sported by that hiker happened to match the ones inked on the necks of all his capos.

I go with my gut and kill the lights. A flash of red darts out from the shadows of thick woods—brake lights—a crimson pixie leading me to *Bella's* precise location.

And by pixie, I mean evil little bitch.

Between Kennedy and me lies another unforgiving ravine. *Bella* stands on one side, I on the other.

With a step forward, I instantly lose my footing, slipping on damp, moss-covered stones. I latch onto the nearest branch, legs dangling.

It takes me a minute to hoist myself back up, catch my breath, and steady my stance. When the pucker of my ass manages to unclench, I take three large steps away from *el capo's* welcome mat, return to my car, and call for reinforcements.

"Hello?" he answers like an idiot. "Does someone *need* me?"

I quell the beast that wants to lash out with a *fuck off* and breathe through it. "Yes," I growl.

I don't need Dante's help as much as the guy with him. Striker. Technically, my bodyguard.

But since my brothers assigned him to me, I do what I always do when I suspect someone's allegiance is divided. I cut them like bait.

Which is why, with the threat of my brothers likely hanging over his balls like a guillotine if he loses me again, he's with Dante. And armed with his night vision goggles, because, let's face it, the freak's never without them.

"Well, cell reception is shit out here and we can't get a lock on your location. Where are you?"

I'm two seconds from firing off a flare when I make that evil little pixie my bitch. I slide behind the wheel and pump the brakes.

For what feels like forever, I stand there and wait. By the time the roar of Dante's engine closes in, I've flipped through every image of torture I've ever seen in my life.

My fingers curl into fists, adrenaline coursing through my veins, fueled by pure primal rage.

Whoever's on the other side of the ravine is about to be skinned and made into a motorcycle jacket.

CHAPTER 2
Kennedy

"Y-YOU?" I stammer, recognizing the man. Same greasy, disheveled gray hair. Same unlit cigarette behind one ear, which is just disgusting.

I'd managed to wrestle my hands free from the thick, knotted ropes, only to find myself trapped in a trunk, surrounded by the deafening sound of my own pulse and a riptide of fear and hopelessness.

Shivering, I tightened Enzo's blazer around me. In the darkness, it was easy to breathe him in—his cologne and expensive cigars—and somehow draw strength from him.

I'd almost convinced myself I was ready for anything, steeling myself for what was to come.

But nothing—absolutely nothing—prepared me for this.

Clive Weston. Owner of Weston's Dance Academy. Or, former owner, according to his soon-to-be ex-wife.

He leers at my half-naked body as I scramble to get Enzo's blazer over every exposed inch of my skin.

"Shy?" He chuckles, reaching out to touch my hair as I whip away. "No need to be, sweetheart. I've seen all of that whore body of yours."

This time, he grabs me by the hair as I recoil, cowering further into the cramped space—trapped. I'd rather die than let this man lay a hand on me.

I cry out. "What do you want?"

"Me?" Clive asks, yanking me up and licking his disgusting lips. "I don't want a thing."

Out of nowhere, footsteps crunch from just out of sight. My pulse freezes.

"She's all yours, Mr. Rocco."

Dread tightens my chest as a man emerges from the trees. I know him too, and prayed I'd never see him again.

It's him—the thug from the bar. The man who was seconds away from raping me and nearly shattered my hand.

I escaped him once. But Truffles isn't here this time.

"Surprised to see me, cunt?"

His dark, bottomless eyes are strained red, and by the looks in them, he's high, pissed, and about to pick up where he left off.

Frantic for an escape, I dart a glance around. *Shit*. We're alone. In the woods. Presumably miles from where anyone will hear my screams.

The only thing that would make this any worse is creepy music, duct tape, and a sacrificial altar.

"Where'd you find her?" he asks Clive.

"D'Angelo's club. Dante's Inferno. She was spreading her legs real good for Enzo."

The fact that Clive Weston watched Enzo lick me to heaven

shoves bile up my throat. I have to fight the urge to gag, and swallow hard.

Panic claws at me as Rocco undoes his belt, and tears burn my eyes. He can't do this. Please, God, don't let him do this.

He's three times my size and strong—so goddamned strong. I learned that from our encounter in the alley. *Fuck*, what do I do?

"You can go," he snarls to Clive, but he's so close to me, the stench of rotting eggs and booze nearly knocks me out.

Before he unzips, Clive steps between us, shoving him back with a fierce glare. I almost mistake his move for sanity until he says, "My money first, Rocco. Then you fuck the girl."

Rocco laughs. "What are you, her pimp?"

Clive lunges forward, throwing his weight at him. "Give me my money."

But with a single hand, Rocco shoves him to the ground. "You got this car."

"It's broke," he complains, pointing out the busted taillight. "And that wasn't the deal. You promised me twenty grand," Clive argues, his voice trembling, outraged.

"Be smart, Clive. Just walk away."

Clive is many things, but smart isn't one of them. Despite the fact he's a foot shorter than Rocco and has the physique of a janitor, he attacks, arms flailing.

Rocco smashes the bottle of Jack on the car, shards flying everywhere. In one swift move, he slices Clive's cheek, the broken end now a lethal weapon at his neck. "D'Angelo may have beaten you up over this girl, but you fuck with me, and I'll kill you."

My mind scrambles to process what I just heard. Enzo had Clive beaten up?

For me?

As much as I'd like to luxuriate in that visual a little longer, I can't. Hands up in surrender, Clive retreats, which I'm not sure is a good thing or a bad thing.

It leaves just me with the deranged man licking his lips. Which is a very bad thing.

High on drugs and rage, Rocco seizes my arm. I screech, terror shooting through every part of me as he drags me against his body. "That's it. Scream for me." Tears burn down my face as he slides a hand through my legs.

Then, I hear a sharp crack.

Rocco stops. Staggering backward, his eyes slam shut as he clutches his head. A trail of fresh blood seeps down his face, but his grip tightens like a vise on my leg.

Fueled by adrenaline, I kick his jaw so hard, he's on the ground.

My relief is short-lived when I see Clive panting, a boulder the size of a bowling ball in his hands. His breaths are labored as he clutches his ribs and struggles for air.

I'm not sure if he has asthma or what, but outrunning him might be an option . . . as soon as I'm out of this trunk.

Huffing, he fixes me with a cold stare and cages me in. "Fine. If Rocco won't pay, I'll sell you to Andre. You should fetch a pretty penny, considering you're Enzo's girl."

Enzo's girl?

Images of Enzo flash through my mind like fireworks—his dark features and golden eyes etched against the backdrop of scotch and cigar smoke.

The only man who's ever made me feel alive.

But then, that image fades, replaced by the twinkling eyes and undying spirit of my father. His voice sweeps through my thoughts, blustering with full-throttle Scottish strength.

"*When your back's to the wall, darlin', ya fight.*"

I fight.

I don't think. I act.

A cry erupts from my throat as I unleash a barrage of swift kicks. I aim for Clive's face, but I take what I can get—his gut, his chest, his jaw—until finally, he crumples to the ground like wet paper.

I leap from the trunk and scramble to the driver's seat. *Shit*. No keys.

Desperation and panic grip me as I frantically search the car, then rush back to Clive, scouring his jacket and jeans pockets.

Nothing.

The angry moan of Rocco pierces the air as he starts to stir, groaning. His hand reaches into his pocket, and my heart races as I realize he's going for a gun.

And I run.

Fear sets my direction. Without knowing where I am or which way to go, I bolt through the dark, blind.

Pain slices through every step, my bare feet pounding against sharp pebbles and twigs.

I need to hide. *Now*. Ignoring that unsettled feeling of running in circles and getting nowhere, my feet don't stop.

Then the earth slides out from under me as my body crashes down a hill, slipping against wet moss and twigs. I plunge into the darkness until I plow, full force, into a log.

"*Argh!*" I smother my mouth, my breaths coming out in loud, ragged gasps.

A sharp crack hits the air—a gunshot. And in that moment, reality crashes down on me like a ton of bricks. If I make the wrong move, if I make even the slightest sound, I'm dead.

"Don't make me chase you!" Rocco's shouts. His voice is close. Too close. Footsteps crunch as if they're all around, and I stay painfully still as something slithers against my leg.

"You're only making it worse on yourself," he growls.

He's practically on top of me now. I clamp down on my whimpers, sinking my teeth into my cheek until I taste blood. Any movement, any sound, and I'm dead. Or worse.

And if I don't?

The footsteps move on, then circle back. Once. Twice. Numb with adrenaline before, I didn't feel the pain, but now it crashes over me like a tidal wave. Cold seeps into my bones, making my teeth chatter and my strength worthless.

A cold trail of sweat breaks out along my nape as the footsteps make another pass.

'm terrified. I just escaped the nightmare of those two bastards, and getting caught again isn't an option. Even if they let me live, the things they'll do to me . . .

They'll make me wish I was dead. I know they will.

The chances of getting out of this and seeing Riley, my only sister, or Truffles, my newfound dog, are slim to none.

And then there's Enzo, and whatever the hell he is to me. He's the most hopeless of hopeless causes. So why is my stupid mind clinging to the hard features of his face?

Somehow, it gives me the strength to force my body to kneel, then crawl, making my way painfully slow up the hill.

A branch snaps under my weight, and a rush of footsteps zeroes in on my position. Tears prick the back of my eyes.

The thought that Riley will lose her father and sister and be all alone eats me alive. It's unbearable.

"Keep your word, Enzo," I murmur softly. "Take care of Riley."

CHAPTER 3
Enzo

Fuck, this hill is steep.

It takes us a good half-hour to traverse the ravine. Thirty minutes of navigating through cold, damp, slippery terrain that has me stumbling like a newborn giraffe.

It makes me wish I'd taken the car and left Dante to trek through the woods like a Boy Scout with a compass. But as soon as the brake lights flashed a second time in the distance, it was too late.

Because Dante's right. I am led by my dick.

"Need a hand, sir?" Striker asks, his Neanderthal frame seeming strangely at ease in this rugged environment.

He's managed to find the shallowest passage across. I knew it was here. I just couldn't see it in the velvet pitch-black of a moonless night. Navigating blindfolded would've been easier.

As a child, these woods were a second home. But now, as an adult, my stature and thousand-dollar Italian shoes were about as useful as a wooden condom.

I refuse to grant Uncle Andre or his land an ounce of satisfaction. Or to cling to Striker's hand like a toddler.

"No," I say firmly.

With each ragged step up the embankment, my pulse quickens. *Where is she?* The thought of her body, beaten or unconscious, is too much.

Instead, I entertain the thought of Kennedy hiding and freezing in the dark. As hopeless scenarios go, it seems like the more glass-half-full option.

Once the ground levels out, we picked up to a jog, homing in on the car. With the trunk popped and a faint glow emitting from it, it appears deserted.

We rounded the other side, finding Clive's scumbag body sprawled on the ground nearby, knocked out cold.

My foot nudges a shattered bottle of liquor, and Striker points to the ground. "Blood." The trail disappears into the woods. *Is Kennedy hurt? Or is this from someone else?*

Striker scans the woods. "Do you see her?" I pressed.

He shakes his head.

All my rage erupts as my foot connects with Clive's chest. "Wake up!"

His body curls into a fetal position as he groans.

My vision tunnels, engulfed in red fury. I seize his face, forcing him to meet my gaze. "Where is she, Clive?"

Wincing, he raises both hands in surrender. "It wasn't me. I've been shot," he whines like a pussy.

"Yes. In the arm. Because you're a poor, innocent bystander who happened to be in the wrong place at the wrong time." This time, I kick him so hard I envision that gunshot hole in his arm as my only chance at scoring a World Cup. "Where. Is. She?"

He howls in pain. "It was Andre's man." He begins to sob. "I was trying to help her. Rescue her. I smashed a rock over Rocco's head so she could escape."

I yank him up by the collar and slam him against the car. "You know what I hate more than people who try to mess with me?" I press the barrel of a Glock to his throat. "People who lie about it."

"Enzo, wait!" Dante pulls up, voice cutting through my haze of anger.

It takes a moment for his expression to sink in, for the rush of almost pulling the trigger to subside.

He rushes to my right side, with Striker on my left, both pleading with me not to go through with it, despite the incessant itch of my finger chanting *Do it*.

"Don't kill him," Dante insists.

Seriously? He takes ten years to show up to the party, and greets me with this shit? Which team is he on?

"If you kill him, extracting information from him gets that much harder," Dante says.

Striker holds up his phone. "Besides, sir, Clive is an accountant."

I stare at him like he just fucked a hydrant.

I swear, the fact that Striker is *Big Tony* Santoro's little brother almost doesn't matter. Striker is a moron and needs to be put out of his misery.

Almost is the operative word because Big Tony spent ten years behind bars for the D'Angelos. Our family owes them a debt, not the other way around. If not shooting Striker repays even a fraction of that debt, so be it.

"I can kill an accountant," I mutter dryly.

Striker shakes his head. "He's one of Andre D'Angelo's low level bankers. The dance school was a front for a laundry mat."

Dante says slowly, "He washes money." Each word is enunciated as if I'm slow. He has to nudge me to lower my weapon because I don't want to. "We can use him."

Rambling, Clive pleads for his life. "Yes. Don't kill me. You can use me. I'll spill everything you want to know. Anything." He clasps his hands together in desperation. "Please. I'll even tell you which way your girl and Rocco went."

Dante raises a brow. "I guess everyone knows she's your girl?"

"Shut up." With a resigned sigh, I tilt Clive's chin upward with the gun. "Well, asshole. Which way did they go?"

WE WALK IN SILENCE, COVERING GROUND QUICKLY. Striker, with his ex-military tracking skills, and me, following close behind.

Dante handled Clive. How? Don't know. Don't care. As long as Clive Weston is out of *Bella's* life once and for all, I'm good.

Dante's also happens to be terrified of snakes, but he assured me that had nothing to do chomping at the bit to take care of Clive.

We trudge through terrain so thick, my shoe momentarily

gets stuck. That's when I see it. The crimson pocket square from my blazer, torn against a branch.

Striker moves to retrieve it.

"Leave it," I say.

"You sure?" he asks, uncertainty in his eyes before reaching for it again.

"I said leave it." This time, it's a command. Part of me prefers not to get attached only to discover she's dead.

And part of me—the one currently winning the arm wrestling match—has no use for things. It's just a scrap of fabric. It isn't *Bella*.

He does and moves along. As much as I hate to admit it, Striker's skills are coming in handy. Between stealthily moving through brush and tracking the specks of blood like a hound, we're plowing through this thicket of trees fast.

But it does nothing to quell the emotions rising against my insides like acid and consuming me whole.

Emotions the press credits me with lacking.

The problem is, we're not just looking for Kennedy. We're also hunting down Rocco, my uncle's right-hand man. A notorious loose cannon, his violent streak and insatiable coke habit only add fuel to the fire, increasing the tally of rape victims in Chicago and across the state.

Without warning, all the visuals of Kennedy being served up on a platter to be his next victim explode with uncontrolled force.

Before I can even process what I'm doing, raw anger surges and my fist flies out, connecting with Striker's jaw with a cold, hard thud.

Granted, his face is as hard as Mt. Rushmore and I might

have a few broken knuckles, but I don't let up. "When I say to scare someone, I don't mean to break her fucking hand."

That little nugget—that Kennedy's already injured stirs in my gut like acid. I wanted her to call my goddamned number, not get roughed up by my own hired gun.

Striker doesn't hit back, doesn't retaliate. Instead, he remains eerily calm, a stark contrast to my own state of freaking the fuck out. "I get it. You feel"—he rubs a hand along his chin as if fishing for the right word—"out of control. But for the record, I never laid a hand on her."

I'll show him out of control. I level the gun between his eyes. "Did you or did you not hear me earlier? I hate liars."

Both of his hands raise in surrender. "You said, and I'm paraphrasing, if I failed you, you'd have someone else do it."

I lower the gun slightly. "And?"

"And, by the time I got to the bar, the guy was already roughing her up."

Confused, I try to make sense of what he's telling me when he lays a hand on my shoulder, clearly having lost his goddamned mind. "I get it, boss. You feel overwhelmed." He opens his arms wide. "My therapist says a hug is always the answer."

"A hug is never the answer," I seethe, swatting his hand away. "What guy?"

Now it's him who's staring at me like I just licked an outlet. He points in the direction we've been tracking. "Rocco."

And in that moment, all the pieces of the puzzle snap into place. What if Rocco connected the dots—his brother's torture at my hand and my tangled on-again-off-again obsession with Kennedy? There'll be no stopping him.

Rocco will unleash his vengeance with exacting precision—strike me right where it hurts.

He will torture her.

Rape her.

Destroy her at her core. He will strip Kennedy Luciano of her soul before auctioning off whatever's left.

And with Uncle Andre's power and influence backing him, he'll be unstoppable.

I try to convince myself it will only hurt if I allow it. That it's not too late.

There's still time to peel Kennedy away like a second skin . . . shed her before she scales my defenses, cracks open my chest, and pierces my ice-cold heart.

"Boss?" Striker asks, his voice tentative. "Do we keep going?"

The realization hits me like a bolt of lightning, sparking a volatile mixture of rage and desperation. "Fuck," I grit through clenched teeth.

"Someone's coming!" Striker whispers urgently, his voice barely audible over the rustle of leaves. His eyes beg for direction, silently asking what I want to do next.

Disgusted, I shake my head. I know what must be done.

Without hesitation, I gesture away from the approaching footsteps and point back in the direction we came.

Confused, Striker furrows his brow. "Huh?"

Annoyed, I roll my eyes and snap, "Go!"

CHAPTER 4
Kennedy

"Come on out, little girl," Rocco chuckles, the sound sending shivers down my spine.

My heart races in my chest as I stumble over leaves and slippery rocks. My eyes strain against the darkness, desperately searching for any sign of hope.

A way out.

A place to hide.

A weapon.

Just to be clear, I am not exactly what you'd call a wilderness girl. My idea of camping involves shoving a stick through a marshmallow's butt and toasting it over an open burner. So, stumbling blindly through the darkness can only mean one thing: I'm hopelessly lost.

"You're only making it harder on yourself." His voice grows louder.

The bastard's getting closer, and it takes every ounce of willpower I've got to shove aside the suffocating fear and muster the strength to keep going.

I try to quiet my hurried steps, attempting to calm the loud, frantic rhythm of my breath, but it's no use. The snap of a twig beneath my foot assures me there's no way he can't hear me.

No way he won't find me.

Rocco's ominous voice echoes through the trees. "I'll just send the dogs in the morning."

Dogs?

Morning?

I envision a horde of ferocious dogs, their growls and howls echoing through the chilled morning air as they tear into my frozen solid fingers as the dawn breaks.

I shiver again. I've got to get out of here.

The ink of night begins to thin as I tread toward what seems to be an opening. Suddenly, my footing slips on a slick, mossy bed of leaves, and I crash down. "Damn it."

"I hear you, little bug," he bellows with a chuckle.

To me, this is life or death.

To him, it's all one sick, twisted game.

I squeeze my eyes shut, gritting my teeth against the pain, and press onward. Another slip sends me tumbling. Gazing up to the heavens, I ask Dad, *What do I do, Da?*

"Ya fight, darlin'." Dad's voice echoes in my head like a mantra. *"Fight!"*

Fight my father whispers from beyond the grave, and I nod. Because either I'm listening to him, for once, and somehow surviving this dumpster fire of a night, or I'm joining him.

With a strength I wasn't sure I possessed, I take a cautious step forward, then another, until I stumble against the rough bark of a tree.

Rocco's voice slices through the darkness, a sharp and cruel taunt. "Here, kitty, kitty," he jeers.

I clamp my hand over my mouth, desperate to silence the ragged breaths that betray my hiding place.

His voice fades, teasingly distant. Then, in the next breath, his footsteps shatter the silence, crunching all around, dangerously close.

Fumbling in the darkness, my hand lands on a sturdy fallen branch. Perhaps a swift strike to the head—mirroring the blow to Clive—will buy me the precious seconds needed for escape.

But where to? The soles of my feet scream in protest, raw and shredded from the jagged terrain. And even if I manage to outrun him, it's only a matter of time before he catches up.

Or the dogs do.

When a twig snaps to my left, instinct kicks in.

I swing, hard. Poised for defense, I struggle, when a powerful hand catches the branch mid-air.

Before I can let out a sound—a scream—I'm trapped against the tree, my mouth is covered, my body wedged between solid timber and an unyielding presence.

The rush of panic ebbs away, replaced by an unsettling calm.

The air is thick with the scent of cigars mingling with the faint hint of cologne. The glimmer of golden eyes stare down, illuminated by stray beams of moonlight.

Enzo?

"Shh," he whispers low in my ear. My body settles, motionless beneath his hold. I remain still, pressed against him, every muscle tense and motionless.

Another snap of twigs cuts through the silence, followed by

the thud of heavy footsteps drawing near. My heart races, threatening to burst from my chest.

Then they pick up their pace, and slowly fade away into the distance.

It's only then that Enzo releases me. Even in the dim forest light, his stare is piercing. Without a word, he seizes my hand and pulls me along with so much urgency that I'm left breathless.

The next sharp stone slices into my foot, the pain driving me to my knees. I clench my teeth, fighting back a gut-wrenching cry that threatens to escape.

More noises stir in the distance, prompting Enzo to act. He gathers me up in his arms, cradling me against his chest, as he forges ahead through the shadows.

Overwhelmed by exhaustion and crashing through too many emotions to count, my head sinks into his shoulder.

I want to warn him about the rugged terrain and slick boulders, but he maneuvers through them so effortlessly it's clear he's using The Force.

In this moment, an odd sense of reassurance floods me. With this mafia king turned mountain man leading us to safety, it's as if nothing in the world can hurt me.

Not even him.

Then, just as my body melts into his hold, Prince Charming has to open his mouth. "Where are your shoes?" he mutters, annoyed.

My eyes snap wide. Oh, my God, he can't be serious. "Um, at Dante's Inferno. Where they were left when I was abandoned by you . . . and freaking kidnapped."

"I did not abandon you," he grunts back. "I"—he thinks on

it, finding just the right words—"had important business." Then he adds, "Family business," as if that makes it all better.

My anger frayed, I glare up at him. "You mean like the family business of cozying up to your uncle and telling him I'm a two-bit whore? *That* family business?"

"What was I supposed to tell him?" he asks, as if I'm slower than airport Wi-Fi.

Is that what he actually thinks? That I'm a two-bit whore?

If he wasn't my lifeline right now, I'd flick him in the forehead.

"For the record, I do not *cozy up* to my uncle."

"Strike a nerve, did I?" I ask.

His steps turn to stomps. "Do not push me, Kennedy."

So now I'm Kennedy again. A big, blaring, Do Not Kick the Hornet's Nest warning sign, I guess.

And he's right. I really shouldn't push him. The sane part of me knows this. That this broody, living god is rescuing me.

Despite his hardened jaw and steel behind his eyes, his grip on me tightens. It's like watching an irate toddler stomp through the forest, protecting a precious toy.

Then his frustration snaps. "This isn't working for me." It's as if he's come to a decision. One that suddenly doesn't include me.

What?

My jaw would've hit the ground if Enzo hadn't been hauling me through the woods at a breakneck pace. Like a bull at a rodeo, my Scottish side charges into the fray, full force.

"News flash, Mr. D'Angelo. This—I gesture to my bashed-up body and his ridiculous blazer as my only article of clothing—"isn't working for me either."

Our words hang between us like a challenge, each of us daring the other to back down first. But deep down, I know there's more between us than angry words and pent-up frustration.

And enough raw heat blazing between us to power the sun.

Tension escalates, thick and palpable, as we try—and fail—to keep our voices low. Out of sheer exasperation, I poke the bear. "Why didn't you do what you mobsters normally do?"

"Criticizing my work?" He smirks. "And what is it you think we *mobsters* normally do?"

"I don't know. Shoot him? Like, in the kneecaps or something?"

With the grace of a panther, Enzo effortlessly sidesteps a low-hanging branch, guiding us forward through a pitch-black patch of forest.

"I assure you, *Bella*, there's nothing I'd love more than to put a bullet in his kneecap. Or something," he huffs, his hold on me tightening. "Look around," he prompts.

I do, feeling more lost than ever.

"It's dark. If I fire at him, I might hit you," he adds, adjusting me in his arms as he considers our next move. "And even if by some miracle I managed to hit him, chances are he'd fire back. Which means one of us would be dead. Possibly me," he says, with a touch of sarcasm.

At least, I think it's sarcasm.

Who knows?

There's so much raw tension knotted between us, I'm not sure of anything anymore.

Except that he's rescuing me. And I need to be more

grateful and less *dumping all my pent-up shit* on the man carrying me out of the bowels of hell.

I let out a soft breath. "Thank you," I utter.

"For not killing you myself when you got yourself kidnapped?" I swear, this man needs Jesus.

"Hey." I brush a hand on his cheek. His footsteps slow as his eyes meet mine. "I'm thanking you. For rescuing me, Enzo. Don't be a dick about it."

The slightest grin tugs at his lips. "Don't tell me what to do, *Bella*. And don't thank me yet." After a long moment of huffing and deliberation, he resumes his stride.

We hit a clearing where a car is idling ,and a man rushes up to us. He looks so much like Enzo that I'm momentarily stunned.

"Striker?" Enzo asks.

The man checks his watch. "Returning from the deepest part of the ravine about now." They share a chuckle, and I catch the hint of some inside joke slipping past me.

Enzo nods, pure satisfaction gleaming in his eyes. "I take it back. Striker's not worthless, after all. He makes excellent bait."

They talk as though I'm not even there, and honestly, I'm fine with that. Perfectly content to fade into the background in Enzo's arms—especially since I'm buck naked under the oversized blazer.

But my brief respite from the spotlight is short-lived.

The man shifts his attention to me and speaks. "So, this is her."

I blink. "This is who?" I question.

The man's gaze leisurely drifts over me, a smirk playing on

his lips. "The woman causing all this trouble," he drawls out, his voice oozing allure.

The growl that rumbles from Enzo's chest is primal. Possessive. "That's exactly what she is. Trouble. More than she's worth if you keep eyeing her like a prize cut of steak."

Really? He's claiming me now? Because I'm pretty sure if we stick around much longer, Rocco will find us. Especially with these two going at it like five-year-olds playing tug-of-war over a blanket.

Exasperated, I shake my head. "You can put me down now."

"Considering it looks like your feet have been mangled by a cheese grater, I don't think so."

In truth, he has a point. But what's he going to do? Piggy back me back to Chicago? "I'm a dancer. My feet know pain. Now put me down."

"Fine," he concedes, signaling for the other guy to open the car door, which he promptly does.

But instead of setting me on my feet, he slides me into the back seat of the car. The door shuts behind me, and after a few minutes, neither of them gets in, leaving me to wonder what we're waiting for.

Finally, a man emerges from the woods—someone unfamiliar, with an almost military bearing and reddish hair. He's wearing strange goggles on his face, which he promptly removes.

After a brief exchange, he climbs into the front seat while Enzo's lookalike slides in behind the wheel.

Instead of joining us, Enzo remains behind. As soon as the engine fires up, alarm bells blare in my head. "We can't just leave him."

"He said to go," the military-looking one says.

Enzo's doppelgänger nods. "He said to go." He puts the car in gear and we're off. "Rule number one: Don't argue with Enzo."

Who's he telling?

The car pulls away, and all I can do is look back and watch, helplessly, as Enzo disappears into the woods. We round a dense thicket of trees, and a distinct sound jolts me in my seat.

A loud clap in the dark.

Gunfire.

CHAPTER 5
Enzo

I SCAN THE ROOM, then shoot a look over at Dante.

In my head, I'm thanking him profusely for helping with Kennedy's rescue. Outwardly, I'm shooting a death-glare at him and mentally plotting a dozen ways to kill him in his sleep.

"So, there we were," he begins, recounting last night's chaos. "Striker had just emerged from Uncle Andre's 'Hiker's Trail'"—he air quotes—"NVGs and all. We're all out of the woods, safe and ready to go, and this dipshit decides to head back in."

"Why?" Dillon asks, perplexed. His confusion mirrors the question on everyone's mind.

All eyes pivot to me.

I glance at my watch. Ten in the morning. With zero sleep and a near-blinding headache, I'm in desperate need of booze.

I make my way to the Macallan 25 because it's the only scotch that matters, pour myself two fingers, and sip. I blow out a breath. "I had something to take care of."

"More like you had a death wish," Mateo says.

With Smoke, Mateo, and Dante present, it means Dillon drew the short straw. Mateo holds up his phone, letting Dillon chime in via the FaceTime peanut gallery.

"And you shot someone?" Smoke asks, his eyes darting between Dante and me. "Who?"

Dante jumps in before I get a word out. "The one person Uncle Andre will definitely miss," he says bluntly, then adds, "Rocco."

Mateo shakes his head, his expression grave. "You realize you might have just single-handedly declared war."

I roll my eyes. "I didn't kill him," I retort. "Sadly, he's still breathing."

"I don't believe this." Smoke's jaw tightens, his fingers forming a steeple. "One minute, you've got two half-naked women on your arms, enjoying your birthday party. The next, you're racing to Uncle Andre's, armed to the hilt." He points at my chest. "When's the last time you slept? Or ate?"

I'm about to answer when Dante interjects, "Pussy doesn't count."

"I'm fine" I say, with enough conviction that I almost buy it myself.

"You're spiraling out of control," Smoke fires back.

I toss back the rest of my drink. "You know who can't believe this? Me. Standing here, being lectured like a teenager caught swiping a credit card to buy a room full of hookers."

Dante smirks. "You got more than a lecture for swiping dad's credit card."

Dillon's face fills the screen, shaking his head in clear disappointment. "You seriously shot Rocco," he says, disbelief evident in his voice as he pauses for effect before adding, "Without us?"

We all snicker as frustration deepens Smoke's brows into a tight knot.

Hmm. I probably shouldn't spill the beans about what I did to Rocco's brother, Rot. Especially since Rot's beaten beyond recognition—comatose and barely clinging to life.

Smoke's already edgy as hell, with the wedding barreling towards him like a freight train. Judging by his wary glances darting in my direction and the fact that he's always packing heat, it's best I keep Rot's condition close to the vest.

Besides, I've got him stashed away in a makeshift underground medical facility that's way too good for his sorry ass. For now, he lives.

But once he wakes up, I'll wring that fucker dry of every bit of information he has on our sister. No matter how much he begs for the sweet release of death, he doesn't die until I say he dies.

Especially since he holds the key to finding out who targeted Trinity all those years ago, before her attack.

I glance around the room, briefly debating whether to spill the beans to my brothers.

But what if I'm wrong? It's entirely possible that Rot's as clueless as he looks.

Or what if he dies?

Until I have more to go on, I'll keep it to myself. Let them think I've done an epic swan dive off the deep end.

Better they believe that than raise their hopes again, only to have them crushed.

Mateo's eyes narrow as he reads me like a book. "You"—he jabs a finger at my chest—"have a girlfriend?"

"I do not have a girlfriend."

"Are you sure?" Dillon asks, just to rile me up. "Because if your girl's worth going to war over, we have to meet her," he says with a suggestive smirk.

"She's not my girl," I lie, hoping to shut down this conversation from hell.

But who am I kidding? I fingered her, ate her out, and mounted a half-million dollar search mission just to get her back. I also got my hands dirty and rescued her myself rather than waiting twenty minutes for professional reinforcements.

So, yeah, of course, she's mine.

Plus, nothing says possession like shooting an asshole for touching her.

I just don't want any of these dickheads sniffing around her and forcing me to kill them.

"So, she's up for grabs?" Dante adds with a smirk.

"Well, she would be, if you had the inclination to grab anything other than your own dick."

Smoke rubs his temple, his eyes piercing into mine. "Are we seriously going to war over this girl?"

Are we?

My jaw tightens, and a tight knot forms in my throat. Debating the issue is pointless. I simply say, "No."

"Then fix it," Smoke commands, nodding toward the door. "Before I start handing out combat gear at the wedding reception."

I glance at my brothers. Their loyalty and readiness to fight for me evident in each of their faces.

It doesn't matter how deeply *Bella* slips under my skin, my family comes first—now and always. The thought of losing any of them over—what? An infatuation?—is unbearable.

With a firm nod, I steel myself and head purposefully towards the door. "Fine. I'll fix it."

FROM A WEATHERED BENCH NESTLED WITHIN THE tranquil embrace of the church grounds, I set out to "fix it." What better way than by killing two birds with one stone?

The first bird: Uncle Andre.

The scent of age-old stone mixes with the faint aroma of incense, accompanied by the soft rustle of leaves dancing in the breeze. And for one brief moment, I almost forget how much I want to carve out his spleen.

As soon as he speaks, my fists involuntarily clench, a reflex to his words. "I'll give you the girl," Andre says.

My gaze falls to his impeccable Armani suit, destroyed by a garish bright red shirt and puke-green suspenders. It's as if his sense of style came straight out of a bad mafia film.

Either that, or he's actually color-blind.

I gesture toward his attire. "Just because you dress the part doesn't make you Santa Claus. What do you really want?"

"Isn't it obvious?" My stare goes blank. He adds, "I want you back."

"Back?" The word comes out stilted and stunned, though I quickly regain my composure. "I think instead of *back*, you meant to say *dead*. You want me dead."

He shakes his head, chuckling in that way he always does

when he thinks he's in control. "No matter how much you betrayed me, I still see you as a son."

His words grate on me like jagged glass against bare skin. *Betrayed him?*

The lowlife is responsible for my father's disappearance and my sister's attack. I just have to prove it.

I suck in a breath. "And exactly how do you want me back?"

"The feud between us is senseless." His laugh borders on condescending. "If we don't work together, the fate of your family will only get worse."

Another threat. Shocker. "What do you propose?" I grate out, trying to sound somewhat intrigued.

"Make me CEO of D'Angelo Holdings, and I'll give you anything you want."

"Anything I want . . ." God, it would almost be worth it because I really want to throat punch the fucker. I let that vision swim around my head for a minute before I reply.

The problem is I know what he wants, and being CEO of D'Angelo Holdings is just the tip of the iceberg.

The real issue lies in his insatiable greed, and I don't mean money. Fuck, anyone can have money. Money is the falsest of false idols, and it took Uncle Andre half a lifetime to realize that.

What he really wants—and what's been out of reach for him for fifty long years—is power.

Power is an aphrodisiac of epic proportions. A drug of unparalleled potency—the ultimate high. And the more I possess, the more he'll have to pry it from my cold, dead hands before he gains an iota of it.

When I say nothing, he goes on. "I've always admired the

view of the Chicago River from Antonio's office. Or should I say, *your* office now?" His sneer twists into a snarl as he speaks. "Just one of the many perks of your father's disappearance." Leaning closer, he nods with a smirk. "Spectacular views."

My blood simmers beneath the surface, and it takes a long, meditative breath to lull it back. I remind myself that revenge is like a fine, aged whiskey—the flavor only deepens with time.

And when the moment for retribution finally comes, the taste of my vengeance will be unparalleled, rich, and lingering.

I let a grin play on my lips. "I could make you CEO," I suggest, stroking my chin as if giving it serious thought. As if I would even consider handing over the reins to my father's empire—his legacy. "Or..."

"Or?" he asks, interested.

"Or I could just lead you to the panoramic balcony of my office and send you plummeting a thousand feet to the pavement below," I suggest casually, relishing the shock that flickers across his face. "Spectacular views."

With a furious flick of his fingers, he snaps. The echo of footsteps begin from down the corridor.

Given my arrangements with the church, I half-expect Father Malone to round the corner. As a devout and trusted agent of God, he's become the quintessential consigliere to both camps—a role no one else can claim.

And, considering Uncle Andre's ticket to hell was bought and stamped ages ago, it's odd that his donations to the church still rival mine. As if he can buy his way out of eternal damnation and into the pearly gates.

I'm not easily fooled or insanely delusional. Sins don't

exactly pile up on their own, and I don't pour millions into this church for absolution.

For starters, my sins are too dark, too damning. They've earned me a place in hell that's probably ten times hotter than Uncle Andre's, and I've earned every scorching degree.

They tilt the balance in favor of every mother, child, and Trinity out there. A fighting chance to continue the goodness my father endeavored to leave behind.

And a colossal *fuck you* to my uncle.

The footsteps draw near, and I check my watch. *Right on time*.

But it isn't Father Malone's measured steps that come into view.

It's Rocco's.

CHAPTER 6
Enzo

Rocco's growl cuts through the air. "Well, well, well. Look what the cat dragged in."

His slicked-back hair, oozing with grease, only amplifies the roundness of his face. And that defiantly unruly unibrow adds to the effect, sharply accenting the scowl etched across his face.

As my gaze settles on his thickly bandaged hand, a warm sense of satisfaction washes over me. A smile, impossible to suppress, tugs at the corners of my lips.

"That looks like it hurt," I quip. "Must be a real bitch to jerk off with."

"I guess I'll just have your girl do it for me."

My gaze locks with Rocco's, a silent challenge passing between us, daring him to make a move. One move—any move—and church or no church, I will end him.

Before I add a bullet hole to his head to match the one in his hand, Andre plants himself between us. "You know the rules, Enzo," he says, as if I'm new to the game. "Luciano owes me, therefore the girl owes me. No one and nothing can erase that debt. Only I have that power."

His words bear down on me like dead weight, but I stand my ground, easily towering over both of them. When I finally speak, my voice comes out flat. "Thanks for the lesson in Crime Boss 101."

Uncle Andre doesn't ease up. "Don't bother pretending Jimmy Luciano's daughter doesn't mean something to you," he says, his tone softening just slightly. "I know she does."

Taking a slow, deep breath, biting back the inclination to say *stepdaughter*. It would tip my hand and expose just how interested I am.

I try to steady my racing pulse, tuning in to the soothing rustle of leaves and the playful chirping of nearby sparrows.

Kennedy has somehow slipped her way past my defenses and into the heart of my dark world. Cutting her loose would be like tossing her over the fence into Uncle Andre's backyard—straight into Rocco's sadistic playground.

Instead of reacting—admitting or denying anything at all, I pretend that whether Kennedy Luciano lives or dies doesn't matter. "Get to your point."

He pulls out a vial from his jacket, returning to his seat with a grin. Tapping half the coke on the backside of his hand, he extends the rest towards me.

I refuse with a bored wave, and he tosses the remainder to Rocco, who eagerly snorts it up, leaving a trail of snot all over his hand.

Fucking gross.

"I made you, Enzo," my uncle says. "Or have you conveniently forgotten?"

The scars etched across my arms, chest, and back serve as constant reminders. How could I forget?

With narrowed eyes, Uncle Andre cuts through the bullshit and gets to the point. He presents it like a fine meal, with my head as the main course. "Join me," he says, "and Kennedy's debt is yours."

And there it is. What he really wants.

Me.

Indebted to him.

Kennedy's life for mine.

Like butter melting under the midday sun, my composure begins to dissolve beneath his watchful gaze. The tension in my jaw, the hardened glare I suddenly can't shake, the stabbing pain at the base of my neck—every tell betrays me, at the worst possible time.

My emotions swarm like angry bees, relentless and fierce within me. Battling them one by one? Manageable. But facing them all at once? It's like wrestling with a beast, powerful and desperate for action.

I hate that my uncle knows her name.

I hate hearing those three perfect syllables marred by the edges of his mouth.

But above all of that, I hate this. The effect she has on me.

Just hearing her name in this conversation has my pulse racing like a snare drum at a halftime show, and it's infuriating.

It's as if that dark, inky void in the center of my chest suddenly feels a glimmer of warmth and is gravitating towards it.

As if a life without Kennedy Luciano is nothing but a lie.

Fuck.

Who am I?

I meet Uncle Andre's expectant gaze, his eyes boring into mine as if searching for my reaction. "Well?" he prods, his voice a low rumble, almost soothing.

If this were anyone else, I'd tell him to grab a bottle of lube and go fuck himself.

Instead, I straighten my sleeve and shrug. "From what I've heard, the Luciano girl has enough to buy off Jimmy's debt and then some."

Uncle Andre's lips tighten, a smirk curling at the edges. He leans in. "Not if a single dollar of it came from you." His words cut through me like a knife.

He's got me. Got my goddamn balls in a vise, and he knows it. It's like I'm standing beneath the five commandments of the underworld, getting sledgehammered over the head by them.

1. Family first;

2. Death to our enemies—*how swiftly and severely they meet their end is a matter of personal preference, limited only by one's imagination, appetite for violence, and time allotted;*

3. Betrayal warrants swift consequences—*with similar creative license as number two;*

4. Snitches get stitches—*which, despite its lack of originality, remains a steadfast truth;*

and last but not least,

5. Debts *will* be honored.

No one eats, sleeps, and breathes these laws more than I do. And right now, the last one is coming back to fuck me in the ass.

The D'Angelos set the rules, and once established, they became gospel.

When our family split, each king dictated his own laws, his own brand of justice—no questions asked.

We don't meddle in the affairs of others, and they damn well know better than to stick their noses in ours.

At least, if they want to keep their faces intact.

The consequences for crossing those lines? Bloodshed and war.

And make no mistake, Kennedy Luciano is worth neither. At least, that's what my brain keeps telling my dick.

For a fleeting second, I wonder if she stands a chance of paying down the debt on her own. Casually, I crunch the numbers in my head.

Hell, I don't even have to carry the one. For all that asinine *work-herself-to-death* nobility, she's barely scraped together ten grand.

Which is admirable. Too bad she owes ten times that amount.

Which means I'm either gearing up for battle or I'm tossing her to the wolves and drowning out her cries as I move on with my life. Uncle Andre's pleased gaze meets mine. "Well?"

I tap a finger on my tailored slacks. *Well, indeed.*

If I had a diplomatic bone in my body, I would smile and nod, allowing my uncle to cozy up to my good graces like a boa constrictor. It would be a cozy scenario, where I could have my fingers in all the pies... especially *Bella's*.

But there's the rub.

I am many things... a bastard? *Yes.*

An alleged womanizer? *Absolutely, though admittedly, it's been a while.*

A lethal thug? Or, my personal favorite, the devil incarnate? *Guilty as charged.*

But a master diplomat? Definitely not.

I'm more of a shoot first, discuss later kind of guy, as evidenced by Rocco's hand.

No, my expertise registers on a darker scale—from broken bones to a gun to the skull, all of which I'm fantasizing about now as Uncle Andre speaks.

As I take my sweet time considering his offer—partly to annoy him, and partly because I'm genuinely contemplating my options—he sports a smug grin. "Come on, *son*. Say yes and spare me the misery of having to sell your little sex toy off to the highest bidder."

The word *son* hit me like a *slap*, and my pulse kicks up. I tamp it down and say nothing.

When I still don't reply, he adds, "If we go to war, my first order of business will be to have Antonio declared dead. You'll lose it all anyway."

Ice crystallizes along the walls of my chest, squeezing all the air from my lungs. Losing our father is not an option. Not like this.

Five years ago, my brothers and I made a pact. Until

Antonio D'Angelo's lifeless body is presented at our feet, he is alive. Period.

That glimmer of hope that he might still be out there keeps us going.

Keeps *me* going.

In the flurry, my mind is bombarded with bright red warning signs, which I promptly ignore. In an instant, the barrel of my Glock finds its place against my uncle's chest. Through gritted teeth, I seethe the threat. "Do it, and your death certificate is next."

But as swiftly as I act, Rocco's gun is pressed to the base of my skull.

Uncle Andre chuckles, diffusing the tension by waving off his attack dog. "There's no reason for family to fight, Enzo. Join me," he offers again.

I ease back the gun a fraction. "I feel like I've seen this movie before," I scoff, the comparison hitting too close to home. "The dark lord asking the young Jedi to join the dark side?" I scoff again. "Yeah, me, too. And even then, all I could think was, *'Fuck that guy.'*"

Andre's smile sinks.

With a smirk, I return the gun to its holster beneath my blazer. "I already have plans to join you," I tell him. "In hell."

All amusement evaporates from his expression as his lips form a hard line. "So be it. Then there's the pressing issue of your little girlfriend."

"She's not my girlfriend," I correct, annoyed. Why does everyone have to put labels on my obsession?

"Oh, good," he replies. "Then you won't mind if I settle her debt by selling her for pennies on the dollar . . . to Rocco."

Rocco's twisted grin erupts in a chuckle. "I'm gonna have a great time teaching your little pet how to take it in the ass for me." He slaps me twice on the cheek.

There's this pinch point within me. A rush that floods in so swiftly and sweetly that it's impossible to see straight. It blurs my vision, clouds my judgment, and tightens my rage into one big, brutal release.

Without warning, my fist flies into Rocco's face so hard his body goes crashing into the fountain, chasing off birds in a frenzy of startled chirps and fluttering wings.

With all three hundred pounds of Rocco hitting it at once, I'm genuinely stunned he didn't break the damned thing.

Seconds from laying another blow to his ribs, he spins around, letting the barrel of his gun catch me right in the gut.

After a long moment of wondering if I can get another punch in before he pulls the trigger, my uncle steps closer and pockets his hands. "Her debt is due tomorrow. But I'll give you one week to decide, Enzo. Before I sell her off."

I say nothing as he eases Rocco's gun aside and helps him to his feet.

"A week?" I ask, and I can't believe I'm actually considering his offer because I know there's a price.

There's always a price.

He nods with his trademark sadistic grin. I take a meditative breath. "What do you want?"

He holds up a finger. "One."

His eyes dart from me to Rocco. Or rather, to Rocco's hand. And I know what exactly what *one* he wants. Payback for putting a bullet through the fucker's hand.

Dante's words come back to me like a warning. "*Get it*

through that Swiss cheese brain of yours. If you get hit—even once more—"

But he's only asking for one. Just one. Rocco. Unleashing his King Kong of a man on me, *manno a manno*. Or rather, gorilla man versus me, with both hands tied behind my back.

My uncle knows as well as I do that I can't let the fight drag out. My thick skull can only take so many hits before I'm back in the hospital. Or worse, the morgue.

But if it means Kennedy gets a week of peace, free and clear, where she doesn't have to look over her shoulder and Rocco stays away, I have to do it.

Ignoring the voices of Dante, the doctors, and worst of all, my own common sense, I agree with a single nod.

I can do one, right?

For *Bella*? *I would do anything.*

Fuck . . .

I should be put out of my misery just for thinking that.

It's a deliberate move—no defensive posture, just letting my arms hang loosely at my sides. Fighting it will only make it worse, so I give in.

Seriously, what's the worst that could happen, right?

Standing tall, chest out, chin up, I fix my gaze on Rocco and the Glock still clutched in his hand. His good hand.

The elusive Scottish brogue that's haunted me for half my life returns out of nowhere, with a vengeance. Sometimes, he's the voice of courage. Other times, the voice of madness.

This time, he comfortably straddles both, rushing straight out of my mouth before I can stop it. "Well? What are you waiting for? Do it!"

And just like that, Rocco strikes. His hand moves in a blur, connecting with my face, but strangely, I feel nothing. No fear, no pain—just a serene calmness washing over me.

Pure and utter peace.

The way it always happens when my world goes black.

CHAPTER 7
Enzo

I DRIFT in and out of serene inner peace when suddenly, a voice shatters the silence. "That's enough!" Firm, unyielding, and unmistakably Father Malone.

A few more minutes of shuteye would've been nice, considering that my lull to consciousness is met with a surge of agonizing pain.

Eyes closed, I gingerly reach for my jaw, wincing as I feel the swelling. It's throbbing, and I might actually need a doctor. Or, at the very least, a dentist.

I pry open an eye, the effort amplifying the pain from mildly tortuous to excruciating agony.

To be clear, I can take a punch. I've been fighting men twice my size since I was fifteen. But the force of two pounds of steel, backed by a three-hundred-pound ape-man's punch, has suddenly taken its toll.

"Can you stand?" Father Malone asks, coaxing me up.

A resounding *"No!"* screams out from the depths of my

soul. But my pride duct tapes that guy's mouth shut and shoves him into the trunk.

Punching through crashing pain and licking blood from my lip, I nod, gritting my teeth as I breathe through it. My head explodes as Father Malone helps me to my feet.

I watch as Andre and Rocco exchange smirks as they turn to leave. And a surge of emotion ripples through me like a sudden gust of wind, stirring the air around us with a dizzying, almost tangible force—the need to kill them.

Not figuratively. Literally.

I know it's a visceral response—a primal instinct deep within me that rails against pain, against the antagonizing thought that if I lose, they win.

This dance is getting old. The one where Uncle Andre is my wrangler, and I'm his wild stallion chained to a post, kicking and bucking until exhaustion sets in and my spirit is stomped out.

I'm not fifteen anymore. And sooner or later, this has to end.

With one of us dead, no doubt.

A weaker man might have crumbled, willing to say or do anything to end the torture. But not me. I simply endure it, familiarizing myself once again with the metallic taste of blood and redirecting my pent-up aggression elsewhere.

My fists clench tightly at my sides, and my jaw tightens as I struggle to regain my composure. I shove Father Malone against the nearest wall, the frustration boiling inside me. "You let Rocco in here," I growl, spitting a mouthful of blood onto the ground.

"All are welcome," he replies, unbothered by my hurling him into a brick wall. "It's literally written at the entrance."

Like all my outbursts, he takes it in stride. Marc Malone, once a prizefighter who could've easily gone pro, stripped his DNA of all inclinations for violence long ago. A subject he often revisits in one too many sermons.

Which means he's here for me.

Because he's under the insane impression that my body needs protection and my soul can be redeemed.

On both counts, he's wrong.

Part of me still needs to lash out, but as the world whirls all around in a dizzying blur, all bets are off. *Fuck. Do I need a hospital?*

With a deep sigh, Father Malone gently guides me to the nearest bench. "You're the one who insisted on having this meeting here. I complied and stayed out of sight."

He wets a corner of his robe from the fountain and gently dabs my face. I wince from the initial blinding pain, which thankfully subsides.

"Keep it up," he says, "and your brain will be pummeled like Play-Doh." I try to pull away, but his iron grip on my chin refuses to release.

"I'm fine," I growl.

"You're suicidal is what you are," he declares as he finishes cleaning me up and inspecting me thoroughly. "But alive. For the moment." He holds up two fingers in a V-shape. "How many fingers?"

I flip him the bird. "One."

He chuckles. "Fine motor skills *and* humor. Good to see your mental processes haven't completely turned to mush."

"I said I'm fine," I snap, then press. "How many?"

His warm smile holds as he nods. "Fifty."

Pride floods his features, but the number pisses me off. "We were aiming for three times that. A hundred and fifty."

"It's a marathon, not a race." His hand rests reassuringly on my shoulder. "Fifty women and children taken from Andre's grasp to safety, right under his nose, was a win, Enzo. More than your father could've accomplished. You should be proud."

Ignoring his last comment, I refocus on the task at hand. "And the rest of them?"

"We'll stagger them in two waves. One next week and one the week after," he explains. "If we move too many at once, the capos will catch on."

"And if we move too few, some will die."

"You can't save them all. Not today, at least," he reminds me. With a plastic cup from a stack by the fountain, he fills it. As kids, we'd drink straight from it. Today, even in the cup, I'm a little skeeved out.

With enough convincing, I sip as he takes a seat beside me. For a moment, I just breathe. "This courtyard is almost a retreat—without the benefits of lavender-scented, half-naked masseuses."

"Considering your money transformed it from a heap of trash, I'd say anything is possible."

I notice the idyllic grin across his face and scold him. "Why, Father Malone. Fantasizing about half-naked masseuses? Shouldn't that earn you at least a timeshare in hell? With you being married to God and all."

"Not exactly God," he corrects, deflecting with a teachable

moment. "The church. The bride of Christ," he explains, using any excuse as a Sunday school teachable moment.

"Whatever."

"And I wasn't fantasizing. Not entirely, anyway." He chuckles, a twinkle in his eye. "I was remembering you and your brothers as kids. If you weren't pounding the Smith boys, you were knocking the crap out of each other."

I chuckle as the memory replays in my head. "Their mom was a saint. Twelve boys. Now, they all work for me."

He turns to me, puzzled. "All of them?"

"Protection for Trinity," I say wearily. "And if you jumped into the line of fire just to make sure I keep your secret, you can relax."

It's no surprise that a former heavyweight would take on fights to keep up his skills.

The fact that he's doing it for cash might ruffle some feathers with the patrons, not to mention the church.

Which boggles my mind. It's not as if he's granting absolution to prostitutes by getting blowjobs, which is definitely how I would abuse my power.

Besides, he donates all his winnings to the church, for which he should be commended, not condemned. It's part of the reason why I've started stuffing the donation box.

That, and the fact that he helps provide safe passage for women and children escaping abuse through old prohibition tunnels right below the very spot we're sitting.

For a beat, his stare pierces through me, assessing. Then, somehow satisfied, he nonchalantly reaches into my blazer pocket and retrieves two cigars.

"Stealing, too?" I quip, feigning surprise.

He hands me one, then takes the other for himself. "This way, you'll stop stuffing them in the collection box with all that cash," he remarks, shaking his head in disgust. "Seriously, I put these in my mouth, and who knows where that cash has been."

With a grin, I twirl the cigar between my fingers. "Oh, I have a pretty good idea."

"Exactly what I was afraid of." He reaches into his robe for a small book of matches.

I recognize the print. "Seriously? Dante's Inferno? Was it priest night at my brother's club?"

He chuckles, flicking the flame to life and igniting each cigar with deliberate care. "You left them in the confessional with your, ahem, 'girlfriend,'" he says with air quotes and a knowing smirk.

"She's not my girlfriend."

He nods. "So you vehemently denied to your uncle." When I stay silent, he adds, "So, you've set your sights on Kennedy?" I puff my cigar, refusing to answer. He exhales a sigh, shaking his head. "You need to be careful, Enzo. She's been through enough."

Great. Just what I need. A sermon.

The man's God-given superpowers include rote memorization of the Bible, spotlighting every last one of my sins, and doling out lectures like candy on Halloween.

And, of course, he knows Kennedy. He's a priest. He knows all the saints and sinners in this godforsaken town. And as much as I appreciate his protectiveness of sweet *Bella*, the last thing I need is advice from Mr. Virgin of the Year.

Kennedy needs to be unleashed, not restrained. Though I could kill two birds with one stone . . .

"There's something you should know about her—"

Instantly, I shut him down. "No, there isn't."

"All right, all right," he concedes, both hands raised in surrender. After a tense pause, he probes, "How is Trinity?"

I blow out a long string of smoke. Damn, I need weed for this conversation. "Better in some ways," I reply vaguely, avoiding his hopeful gaze.

Instead of answering for the millionth time if she remembers him, I take another long drag and let the cigar ease the pain pulsing from my face.

She doesn't remember how close they were.

Or that for a stretch of years between age one to the day she was attacked, Marc was a staple at Sunday dinners—one of us. Grayly defined somewhere between best friend and brother.

Or that he kept vigil by her bedside all sixty-five days in the hospital—until she finally opened her eyes and screamed, terrified at the stranger by her bedside.

I half wonder if it's the reason he turned to God. An offering—sacrificing his true happiness for hers.

Despite all that, he still believes in miracles. That by some wild stretch of the imagination, any day now, all those erased memories will miraculously resurrect themselves.

Hell, the real miracle will be if he comes to terms with her mind being riddled with big, gaping holes.

For whatever reason—delirious pain in my head, perhaps—I toss him a bone. "She's chatty," I offer with another puff from my cigar.

Even from my periphery, I see his eyes light up. "That's good," he says, nearly in tears. "Can I do anything to help?" The hope in his tone is like a hunting knife to the gut.

So before our little chat gets to the point of me feeling the serrated tip of that blade pressing against my sternum—then, heart—I stand.

I let the cigar slip from my fingers to the ground as Father Malone rises alongside me.

Even in my thoughts, he's become "Father Malone." The closeness I feel to him right now means I need to keep distant. For both our sakes.

My steps hasten as he escorts me to the door. As we move past the tall columns, he says, "This is where the two of you met, isn't it?" I pause for a beat. "Though you called her something other than Kennedy."

Bella, though I keep that to myself.

The memory rushes through me, redirecting my thoughts like a trade wind. Kennedy was fiery and raw, untouched by any hint of makeup. And only one word can come close to capturing her in that moment: stunning.

My gaze drifts upward to the ceiling adorned with angels and devils locked in eternal struggle. *Bella* was perfection, with her dark eyes and plump pink lips, subtly parted in awe as she stared up at them.

But then she lost her damned mind and made a scene. That cute little shove she made at my chest imprinted on me.

Owning her was my only option.

I was so tempted to pin her against this very column and teach her a lesson. A good, hard lesson . . . regardless of how many parishioners died of heart attacks at the sight.

Father Malone interrupts my fantasy with a gentle hand on my shoulder, his voice coaxing. "Remember, Enzo, God always has a plan, even when we cannot see it. Trust in His wisdom, and He will guide you through these troubled times."

He's actually talking about Kennedy. And all I can think is . . . *Really? Now you're gaslighting me?* "If God's plan is to have Kennedy violently raped by the likes of Rocco, then yes, Father, His plan is going swimmingly."

Father Malone gasps, stunned, before his expression melts with compassion. Despite the harshness of my words, his gaze is unwavering. "I'm always here for you, Enzo. For even in our darkest moments, His light still shines, guiding us toward redemption."

I grit my teeth against the tide of conflicting emotions swirling within me, grappling with the weight of Father Malone's words.

"Redemption," I echo bitterly, the word tasting like cheap cigarette ash on my tongue. "Tell me, Father, where is the redemption for those who have been wronged, for those who have suffered at the hands of sewer scum like Andre and Rocco?"

Father Malone's gentle eyes meet mine in silent acknowledgment. "Redemption comes in many forms, Enzo," he replies softly. "It is not for us to question God's plan, but to trust in His mercy and His justice."

My resolve hardens like steel as I stare through him into the distance. "God can take the mercy," I reply. "I'll take the justice."

"So you're saving her? This girl, Kennedy?" His eyes light with the idiocy of hope. Or, shit, is it pity?

Because *saving her* is what I would be doing. Sparing her

from a life of beatings, torture, and rape, until the day finally comes when they've had their fill.

At which point what remains of her would be either sold off or dead.

I swallow back the bile churning up from my gut. Father Malone knows better than anyone who I am. The enemies I've amassed. The rules I've vowed to live by.

I want Kennedy. But wrestling her from Uncle Andre's sharp talons would cost more than I have.

I can't trade her safety for the safety of Trinity. Or my brothers.

La famiglia prima. Family first.

Rather than cling to illusions or miracles, I settle into the ice-cold reality of my life, and stare at him like he just jerked off into the fountain behind us.

Slowly, I shake my head. "Kennedy and I made a deal, one which I'll honor. Protect her sister and avenge her father's death."

"If God put her in your path, do you really think you can let her go?"

"I've let lots of women go." Though most try to hang on like a bad case of jock itch. "Letting go of women has never been my issue," I remind him as much as myself.

"You've gotten everything you ever set your sights on, Enzo. Do you really think you'll be able to let her go?" His question hangs in the air like a piñata waiting to be beaten down.

My eyes narrow on his. "Yes," I say firmly. I'm taking a week. Not proposing marriage.

The feel of *Bella's* tight, wet pussy up and down my shaft

just might be worth the cheap price of Rocco's sucker punch—but that's where I draw the line.

With Father Malone's stupid doe-eyed stare boring into my skull, I add, "She had her chance. I offered her anything," I spit. "Cash. A blank check. She chose her sister's life over her own."

"Wouldn't you do the same?"

What kind of a stupid question is that? "Of course, I would," I snap. "And I'm doing it now. You heard Andre. He's hungrier than ever for power, and I'm probably the only thing standing between him and my family's total annihilation. Kennedy's debt belongs to him, and there's nothing I can do about it."

"Can't you?"

"You think I haven't tried?" I gesture to my face. "Hello? How about you let me handle Kennedy, and you do what you do best." I pull out a wad of bills from my pocket and thrust it into his hands. "Focus on your little charity cases."

Thirty grand should shut him up. At least for a while.

He studies the money for a moment, stunned silent. But then he gets his second wind. "Do you know how many people this will help?"

All except the one I want. "I don't care," I mutter.

Then, as if our bond needs more reinforcement, he adds, "The last money you donated went to—"

I hold up a hand, too engrossed in the jackhammer inching its way into the center of my skull to care. "Spare me the details."

He nods, but before my feet clear the exit, Father Malone's grip on my arm stops me like a vise. "Doesn't it bother you that Andre is so interested in this girl?"

I blink. It's as if he hasn't heard me at all.

He steps in front of me. "The man buys and sells debts every day."

"Any man who's seen Kennedy would be interested in her," I explain. "Unless, of course, you're gay, blind, or a priest."

Between my pounding head and me dying a slow, agonizing death from this conversation, I need to leave. Now.

"You need to check into that."

What I need is a Xanax.

I try to sidestep him, but he swiftly blocks my path. "Why won't he just sell you her debt?" he presses, his tone urgent enough that my last shred of patience disappears.

I snatch him by his holier-than-thou collar, my voice booming across the stone walls. "Because it's me!" I snap, the words flying from my lips like bullets through all that reasonable logic.

"He's manipulating you," he says sadly, as if he's finally connected the dots.

I glare with contempt. "Then he's a moron," I spit out, my patience razor-thin. "Like the rest of you, he thinks I give two shits whether Kennedy Luciano lives or dies. And just so we're clear," I add, my words slicing through the tension, "I don't."

I bolt from the room and out the door. Nothing is more important than the safety of my family.

Not even her.

CHAPTER 8
Enzo

"Queen of hearts," Mateo utters, surprised at the card Sin just dealt me.

It's as if he's never played poker with me before.

Pissed, his cards go flying onto the pile. Followed by Dillon's and Dante's as they bitch below their breaths.

I sit there, smiling. Not because I'm about to win this hand, with only Smoke left in the game, but because they're all here. In one room. My brothers.

And I know the dangers. After our father's disappearance, we made a pact to never be in one spot—not all of us. But the truth is, despite the risks, I'm too drained to care and too relieved to put up a fight.

And with them surrounding me, their protective presence and animal warmth all around, it's obvious that they're all here for me.

It's also obvious that Father Malone's gossip game is stronger than TMZ's.

Which means I owe him a whole case of cigars because I've

missed them. So much so that most days, the ache in my chest is hard and intense, and it feels like it's crushing me from the inside out.

With a consoling pat on Mateo's back, Smoke grins. "Don't worry. He may have won the hand, but he lost the war with"—he motions to my face—"a frying pan? Or was it your little lady friend?"

"Apparently, he likes it rough," Dillon winks.

And just like that, *Bella* comes to mind, instantly consuming my thoughts.

Would she like it fast and rough? Or torturously slow? I've had sex so many ways and with so many women, the act has become bland and emotionless. To the point where pleasing them has become an afterthought.

Sad, but true.

And yes, I'm a total asshole. So sue me.

Many women have.

But Kennedy stirs something in me I can't quite put my finger on. Or carve out. It's odd because I'm well acquainted with lust, and that's not it. Even obsession somehow falls short.

It's not about her luscious ass or gorgeous, fuckable tits though the glorious thought of riding either of them has me adjusting in my seat. And don't even get me started on the intoxicating scent of her cunt.

It's her lips.

So full, so inviting, begging to be kissed.

And her eyes, deep and mysterious, like two pools of temptation I want to drown in.

And that damn freckle—a taunting little heart-shaped mark

stamped on her neck—teasing me, tempting me to touch it every chance I get.

Facts are facts. I want her.

Even now, I'm crawling out of my skin, starved for one touch—one taste. It's like the damned woman has somehow managed to rewire my desires at their most basic, primal level.

I breathe through the strain in my pants. So, this is what a voodoo hex feels like.

Another flash of her legs spread eagle and my tongue licking up her flesh sends a surge of need through me so strong I grit my teeth.

Out of nowhere, a poker chip flicks me in the nose.

I blink out of my sex-fogged mind to find my brothers and Sin all staring at me.

I straighten up. "What?"

"It's your turn," Sin says.

Dillon leans into him. "Maybe he has a concussion."

Smoke angles his gaze, piercing his crystal-blue eyes at my head as he assesses me. Considering he's got more medical knowledge than anyone would ever suspect, when his brow pinches to a knot, for a moment, a flicker of concern crosses my mind.

Then, with a hint of amusement, he clears his throat. "I'm pretty sure it's nothing. Just his head shoved up his ass," he says, a smirk tugging at the corners of his lips.

I smirk back, ignoring his comment because the jerk is about to pay. Fifty grand should be more than enough to wipe that smug D'Angelo grin off his face.

I push my stack of chips to the center of the table. "Call."

"Damn it," Smoke grumbles, flicking his cards down with a frustrated sigh. I gather my chips, feeling a rush of triumph.

But the satisfaction of winning is short-lived as Smoke takes a leisurely sip of his scotch, pointing a glass in my direction. "You gonna talk, or do we have to pound it out of you?"

All eyes are on me as Dillon crosses his arms, Mateo pounds his fist, and Dante reaches for a baseball bat. Seriously?

And, as usual, Sin simply stands by and watches, likely recording the whole thing for hours of endless amusement. And to make Trinity laugh.

"I'm fine."

"Don't give us that shit," Smoke says, refilling my glass. "You're hurt. So, we're here. Something we agreed never to do unless it was urgent. And"—he holds up his glass—"we're all drinking scotch, which we hate, for you, prick. Now talk."

I drink, hoping glass number three will quell the dull ache suddenly attacking my head. Then, I talk. "Unless I become Uncle Andre's puppet, he'll petition the court to declare our father dead."

Smoke's words come out tense. Strained. "Tell me he can't do it, Sin."

Sin removes his glasses, pinching the bridge of his nose, determined to rein in the frustration bleeding from every line of his face. "The laws of Illinois say anyone can petition the court. But without evidence or a body—" He cuts himself off.

Our father is alive. He has to be.

Dillon's fury explodes as his fist slams into the pile of chips, sending them flying across the room. "It's bad enough that our father's missing. But if he's declared dead—without a body—we'll lose every ally we have."

"We own half of Chicago," Smoke argues. "And our international footprint covers most of the globe. They can't just pick us off, one by one."

"You mean unless we all become spineless, ball-less doormats," Dante spits out, swinging the bat through the air with a sharp whoosh. "Like Enzo."

"Then you've got nothing to worry about since I'm pretty sure you've been ball-less since birth." I press the cool crystal glass to my head, praying it quells the throbbing.

Sin's patience wears thin. "Yes. That's it. Laugh it up as Andre imagines the next dozen ways he'll demolish this family." His stern gaze falls on me. "None of this explains the condition of your face. With Andre's manicure, I doubt he did that."

I hate what I'm about to say. Mostly because they'll never let me live it down. "It was Rocco."

Dillon's hand flies up. "Hang on. Rocco? The man is slow as dirt. Not to mention you shot him in the hand." Dillon sniffs the air around me. "Someone smells like a big, fat liar. Which means it's about a woman."

Mateo shakes his head. "I distinctly remember Enzo saying we weren't going to war over a girl, and yet, look at him. The battered face of war."

I clench my jaw, frustration bubbling beneath the surface. "It's a complication I'm dealing with," I insist, my voice edged with *stay out of my fucking business*. "I just need a week."

"This girl has an expiration date, does she?" Smoke asks, unconvinced.

"Something like that." When all eyes fix on me, I add, "I'm taking care of it." My features harden enough that this is the point in the conversation they know not to pry further.

Well, everyone knows that but Dillon because he lives to poke the bear. He pats me on the shoulder. "Gonna fuck her and forget her?" He nods in agreement. "That's what I would do."

I glare up at him. "Considering you'd only be pounding two inches of man meat into her, I'm sure it would be easy for both of you to forget."

Smoke raises a brow, suddenly suspicious. "Tell me you're not leaving town."

Leaving town . . . *hmm*. Maybe that's exactly what I need. A little breathing space.

I've been pushing myself to the brink for months, running on fumes. I can't remember the last time I had sex.

I mean, before Kennedy.

Fingering still counts as sex, right?

Assuming it does, that makes exactly twice in the past several months. Twice!

Once in my car as Kennedy's tight little cunt came like Niagara Falls all over my hand. And once when her delectably tight pussy came right on my tongue.

Before I spent my days building empires and my nights taking down the sworn enemies of my father, twice an hour sex was more like it.

I let out a breath, resentment boiling in my veins. I could be having round-the-clock sex with *Bella* right this very minute if Andre hadn't fucked it all up for me.

He called her a *gift*?

More like a curse.

Kennedy was his way of twisting the knife that much more.

And a blaring reminder that whenever his path crossed mine, there were only two ways out...

Death or destruction.

And frankly, destruction was ranking lower and lower each time I had to look at his face.

Which left death.

My uncle has slipped through death's fingers so many times the bastard seems indestructible.

But if I make a move and fail, retribution will be swift and merciless, spelling death for at least one of my brothers, if not more.

I can't afford to lose them.

I study their faces and sip my drink. They're already poised to breathe down my neck and scrutinize my every move. If I stay, they'll hound my every move because they're overprotective and nosy as fuck.

Which means leaving town is sounding better by the minute.

Plus, getting away from Kennedy is less of a bad idea and more like common sense. Everything about her is a distraction.

Doe eyes.

Lush lips.

Juicy fucking tits.

Gah...

I need to create some distance between us, and I need to do it now. For good. "As a matter of fact, I am leaving town," I say, decidedly.

Smoke snaps a stern finger at me. "Now, you listen to me, fucker. My wedding is just around the corner. My bride is a nervous wreck and my future in-laws are twitchy, trigger-happy, and armed to the hilt. They will literally kill me if we go to war."

I chuckle, rubbing my scruff with an evil grin. "So, you're demanding I go to war."

"I mean it," he threatens.

Mateo smacks me in the chest. "At least, don't go to war without us."

"Do I look suicidal?" I ask.

Dante gives me a good once-over. "More like a deranged psychopath."

I hold out a hand his way. "A deranged psychopath who needs a car."

Dante narrows his eyes. "Why can't you use your car?"

"Because Uncle Andre has eyes all over Chicago, and I don't need him stalking my every move."

"What you need is a size fourteen Armani shoe up your ass if you so much as breathe wrong on my two-week-old Aston Martin."

Smoke's phone lights up, playing a music box version of "Here Comes the Bride," and we all roll our eyes as he answers. "Give me one minute, *gattina*." His voice is soft and gushy and so unlike him, I gag.

Smoke places the phone on mute and directs his next words straight at me. "Do not go to war. Do not get killed. And for fuck's sake, don't even think about letting Uncle Andre fist you up the ass until you're his puppet. No pussy is worth that."

"Says the man chasing his own golden pussy around like a whipped puppy," I reply. *Thanks for the visual, by the way*.

Clearly unimpressed, he hardens his glare. "What you and

your dick do with this girl or all the other women on the planet, I don't care. If you're late for my wedding, I'll kill you myself."

"Rest assured, my dick, along with the rest of me, will happily show up on time to hand your ass off," I retort with a smirk.

Satisfied with my response, he downs the rest of his drink and takes off, apparently on call twenty-four seven for his young bride-to-be. Which I suspect is less about fucking her up a wall and more because she's pregnant.

At least, I think she's pregnant with how her tits have blown up like party balloons.

"I can't believe he's marrying her," Dillon says, dumbfounded.

Mateo nods in agreement. "I always thought the only marriage he was heading for was with his right hand." He mimes jerking off as we all snicker.

Sin interjects, his voice slicing through our laughter like a surgeon's scalpel. "Now that Smoke's gone, let's hear more about you, Enzo. And this girl you're fascinated with. Usually, when it comes to women, you have the attention span of a horny squirrel."

"It must be serious," Dante probes.

Once again, all eyes are on me, their curiosity inescapable. I know my brothers. Their questions become a relentless hydra. For each one I deflect, two spawn in its place.

They're hungry for details about why I'm so hung up on a woman, and I'm grasping at those straws myself.

Why am I *fascinated* with Kennedy Luciano?
The hell if I know.

Just as Dante playfully waves the bat at me, a mock threat to *talk, or else*, my phone buzzes. Saved by the bell.

Relieved for a lifeline out of this hellhole before the Spanish inquisition begins, I glance at the screen.

> **STRIKER**
> We have him.

I smile. Thankfully for me, Smoke's appetite for blood has waned. And I need to focus on absolutely anything but *Bella* and the thousand depraved ways I want to devour her.

I reply with a quick text and stand.

> **ENZO**
> On my way

I pocket my phone as my thirst for blood kicks in. "As much as I'd love to welcome you all into the dark corners of my mind, duty calls," I say.

In a rush, I make my way to the door. I'm practically drooling like a werewolf eyeing a lone jogger after dusk. Anything to get away from this.

"Hot date?" Dante needles.

"As a matter of fact, yes. My fist has a date with a man's skull."

Dillon can't resist piling on. "All torture and no sex makes Enzo a dull boy," he tsks.

But it's Mateo who hits me like a Mack truck with his words, stopping me in my tracks. "If she means something to you—anything at all—we've got your back, bro."

He cares.

They all care, and it's suffocating.

The thought of losing them—any of them—because I fucked up and had to have my cake and eat it, too, is too much.

I blow out a breath and say two words, hoping to convince them as much as myself. "She doesn't."

CHAPTER 9
Enzo

SILENTLY, I read from the file. Then, I run through the usual questions. I ask his name or if he has a nickname he prefers I address him by.

Like a moron, he struggles with the zip ties binding his wrists in place. My men have him seated on a chair, wrists cinched to the armrest, with a black sack over his head.

I shake the small pill canister near his ear. He jolts and nearly pisses himself. "Who are you? What do you want?" his voice trembles.

"What do I want?" My words are controlled. "I want... *everything*."

With a nod of my head, one of the guards grabs his finger, ripping it back until the telltale crack hits the air.

An agonized cry rips from his chest. "Stop. Please. I'll tell you anything you want to know." Body writhing in desperation and fear, he's overcome with sobs.

I smack him. "Where's your dignity? For a man capable of such violence... such *hate*... the least you can do is take a little bone break like a man." I lean close to his ear, the smell of formaldehyde and cheap cologne ripe with his sweat. "We still have so many fingers to go."

"No!" he begs at the top of his lungs. "You have the wrong man."

I flip a page, the rustle of the paper loud. He shakes. I smile. "Oh, we have the right man. The pills were your weak point. But that was all greed, wasn't it?" I hold one close to his lips. "Would you like one now?"

The shake of his head is adamant, and his lips form a hard, tight line.

I toss them at his feet. "What's wrong? These magic pills cure every pain imaginable. At first. And what happens the next day? When you don't take them?" His silence crawls along my skin, until I'm agitated enough to backhand him. "Answer me!"

"It g-gets w-worse," he stammers out.

"It gets worse," I repeat as my mouth curls up one side. Getting information will be easier now. Like pressing a button and getting water from a fountain. I breathe deeply, satisfied for the moment, and move on. "Now, let's talk about"—I check the file for the name again—"Anya." The best friend of Smoke's bride.

He screams uncontrollably. "Help! Somebody . . . anybody! *Help!*"

I give him a minute to realize his screams are pointless—wasted energy. Then I continue, torturing him for the next hour before I rip off the bag covering his head.

His eyes are swollen, but not shut. And his face is a mass of blood and bruises. But I want to see his eyes when I say this.

Especially considering that by tonight, he'll never see through those eyes again.

"Look at me!" I snap.

Trembling, he lifts his head until our eyes lock. It's clear he knows now I'm not Smoke. I sport a deadly grin. "Let me introduce myself. I'm Enzo. Perhaps you've heard of me."

It's there in an instant. That flash of fear. The tremors. Once again, my reputation precedes me. Satisfaction heats my blood in a way very few things do.

For a fraction of a second, *Bella's* doe eyes and soft skin flash through my thoughts. I shove her into a closet in the farthest corner of my mind. She can't be here now.

"No." He shakes his head. "Please!"

"*Shh*," I shush him like a child and straighten my cuff. "I have an engagement to attend to, or I'd be able to give you my full attention. But fear not. We'll have more one-on-one time tomorrow." I pull out a syringe.

Panicked, he foolishly struggles with the zip ties again. "What's that?"

"Just something Smoke found in your little stash." I carry on as I hold the needle up to the light. "I've been given every assurance that this little concoction will prolong every sensation." Without warning, I drive it into his neck.

By this point, his freak-out is epic. I'd be freaking out, too, if I were him. His nightmare is only just beginning, and my imagination has so far to go.

"Tomorrow, we'll talk more about my sister, Trinity. You remember Trinity, don't you?" I don't wait for him to lie. I keep going. "Four years," I seethe through gritted teeth, my heart constricting tight. "We lost our sister for four years. Trinity couldn't speak. Or sleep. Or eat, for the most part. Smoke heard nothing but her screams, every night, for four years."

By now, he's weeping uncontrollably. I take a step back to avoid the fresh puddle of urine seeping over to my shoes.

"When Trinity handed an image of the attacker to Smoke, he nearly shit a brick. What luck? He recognized you." I chuckle. "We were idiots, thinking our father's disappearance had anything to do with our sister's attack. We should've been hunting a serial rapist. Especially since all this time, you've been right under our noses."

"I'm sorry!" he wails. "I'll do anything . . ." His words start to slur. A side effect of the medication, I'm told.

"Do? Oh, don't worry. You don't have to do a thing. We'll do all the heavy lifting."

On cue, they hoist the chair up by the legs, letting Mort dangle upside down like a piñata.

I motion to the man with the pliers, instructing him carefully. "Fingers. One knuckle at a time. Stretch it out as long as you can and give him enough water to keep him alive. Leave him like this until tomorrow."

My stand-in smiles like the kindred psychopath he is. "Will do."

I'm about to depart while Striker stands motionless, poised like a clueless statue. Seriously, what the hell?

I've just ripped open a festering wound of a human, and now I'm expected to open my own goddamn door?

I tilt my head and give a pointed cough. "Ahem."

Striker stares past me and gestures. "Something fell out of his pocket, sir. I think it's a photo."

Huh? I pivot around to spot the photo lying too close to

the urine stream for my liking. No way am I getting within ten feet of that mess.

With a mere glance, the photo is scooped into Striker's hand, ready for my scrutiny.

In an instant, apathy makes way for white-hot rage. Liquid fire fills my veins as I free-fall to the center of hell.

I snap up the photo, my fingers trembling with rage as I study it.

My eyes lock on every contour, every line—etching each detail into my brain.

I knew the man I was interrogating had victims, *plural*. They always do. But seeing another photo laid bare in front of me is a wrecking ball to the gut.

Because it's not just any victim I'm staring at in the photograph. It's a girl. A mere child, barely fourteen or fifteen years old at most.

Her eyes, innocent and dark, seem to bore into my soul, pleading for justice that I'm not sure I can deliver.

Every strand of her hair, every delicate sprinkle of freckles on her nose and cheeks, serves as a stark reminder of her youth, her vulnerability. They pave a path down her neck—and to one heart-shaped freckle.

My heart lurches as I stare.

It's Kennedy.

My Kennedy.

Anger boils within me, mingling with a protectiveness I'm not sure I can control. I turn my head to the man dangling by a chain and clench my fists, ready to burn him alive.

I reach for the nearest weapon—a Taser—and strike him center-chest. "Where did you get this?"

He screams in pain, his body twisting, fighting the restraints as he writhes in pain, dangling in the air.

I turn up the dial and hit him again. "Where?"

He passes out.

Frowning, Striker grabs the device from my hands before I can set the dial to max. "Do not make me kill you," I warn.

"You need him alive, sir," he reminds me. "Let us work him over. Go on your vacation. You could use the break."

I glare at Striker, then at the man dangling precariously close to death, and back at Striker.

Deflated, I suck in a breath. Emotionally charged makes for bad torture and even worse information extraction. Plus, I need to save my strength for Clive. Bankers are a goldmine of information. Torturing Clive needs to be a marathon, not a sprint.

I nod, mindless and numb, as I pocket the photo and exit the room. I can't believe I'm even admitting this, but Striker is right.

Ironically, so is Father Malone. God actually does have a plan.

And it's even more fucked-up than I thought.

CHAPTER 10
Kennedy

"ALL RIGHT, EVERYONE, GATHER 'ROUND," I call out, my voice competing with the cacophony of giggles and chatter.

The classroom echoes with the sound of my clapping hands, a futile attempt to corral the attention of the unruly toddlers in the final moments of class.

Tiny bodies bounce and twirl, their tiny ballet slippers executing clumsy pirouettes and wobbly arabesques. Each one a whirlwind of movement, their enthusiasm infectious as they revel in the freedom of movement to Bach.

I weave through the colorful sea of miniature chairs and scattered toys to turn down the music.

My role has morphed from dance instructor to daycare manager. Most of their parents work, and I hate the idea of shooing these little dancers out the door with nowhere to go.

So, I do what I can to provide a safe haven—a place where their imaginations can soar and their spirits can thrive. With juice boxes and oatmeal cookies donated by a local bakery, I try to make their afternoons a fun, happy place that they'll always cherish.

The same way mine was.

When I pitched the idea to the owner, her exact words were, "Do whatever you like. Anything you want."

I should've been flattered, if she hadn't looked oddly terrified when she said it.

Now that I have enough money to pay off Jimmy Luciano's stupid debt, I'm done with that bastard forever. I've quit my other jobs and can finally pursue my passion: dance.

Or rather, pursue my love of dance vicariously through a group of precocious four- to six-year-olds.

Sure, it's the lowest-paying gig in Chicago, and the tips are just gum wrappers and hand-drawn doodles, but it's worth it.

While three squares of ramen a day might sustain my body, but this job feeds my soul.

Again, I clap. "Come on, it's circle time," I coax, gesturing toward the carpeted area at the front of the room.

Amidst the chaos, little Lily is engrossed in a book, oblivious to my attempts to corral the group. I gently place a hand on her shoulder, offering a reassuring smile. "It's time to join us," I say softly.

She holds up the book, and it's one of my favorites. *Angelina Ballerina*.

"How about I read this to the group?" I ask.

"She can't talk," one of the children calls out, and I already know that Lily doesn't speak. Not since her mother passed away.

Her father warned me about how withdrawn she's been,

and it strikes a chord, reminding me of my own struggles after losing my mother.

But like me, Lily loves to dance.

Gently, I stroke her hair. "That's okay," I reassure her softly. "That's what's wonderful about dance. You never need words to express yourself, right?"

Lily's big green eyes meet mine, and when she nods with a shy smile, it's all I need to take her hand and lead her to the group.

As the kids finally settle into place, I take a deep breath and hold up a book. "Can anyone tell me what Angelina's wearing?" I ask.

A chorus of excited voices fills the air as tiny hands shoot up eagerly. "Me! Me! Me!" they exclaim, each child vying for a chance to answer.

I nod encouragingly, pointing to little Emily. "Yes, Emily?"

Emily beams proudly, her face lighting up with excitement. "A tutu!" she exclaims, giggling as she fluffs her own tutu.

"That's right! And what else?" I ask with a smile.

One little girl squeals as she hops to her feet. "Zo!"

Huh?

I whip around to where she's pointing, Enzo's sudden appearance at the door throwing me for a loop.

Despite the fact that he has a black eye and a small gash across his lip—an area I suddenly want to nibble and kiss—he's still gorgeous. Hair mussed to perfection. Jaw carved from stone. Eyes blazing a path down my body.

The man is a god. A living, breathing, brooding god.

Which is unnerving, considering I don't have on a shred of makeup, my hair's a tangled mess, and the dress I'm wearing is a size too small and relentlessly determined to shove my breasts to my neck.

When I offered the kids snacks of peanut butter and jelly crackers, I never imagined my other outfit—a nicely fitting blush leotard and skirt—would be smeared like a napkin.

This dress—one I unearthed from the wardrobe room—was left here when the dance studio was in its prime and a troupe performed *A Midsummer Night's Dream*.

It's elegant, but one of the shoulder straps was completely shredded from the bodice, probably during a particularly challenging scene when Titania seems to float effortlessly, barely supported by her partner.

And the color? A billowy shade of unforgiving white.

It reveals absolutely everything, from the outline of my navel to my now embarrassingly pert nipples. The girls couldn't care less, and the look is common for dance, but as his golden eyes trace a path down my body, I can't help but hold my breath.

Licking my dry lips, I mouth, "What are you doing here?"

Before he can answer, the little girls rush all around him, their eyes wide with delight as they swarm.

I would've half expected him to ask if they were housebroken and worry that they might pee on his expensive shoes. But Enzo surprises me, smiling and greeting them as if they're all long-lost friends.

Then he returns his gaze to me. "I didn't mean to interrupt."

The girls start tugging him by the hands, and patting the floor for him to sit. Which, Enzo Ares D'Angelo, the mafia god of war, actually does.

Without missing a beat, he glances at the book in my hands, points and says, "I see toe shoes."

AFTER TWO MORE BOOKS, THE GIRLS DO WHAT LITTLE girls do in the presence of an attentive adult: They show off.

I put on Taylor Swift's latest song and beam with pride as they all strut their stuff to the beat.

Enzo steps behind me, his breath hot against my ear as he murmurs, "What are they doing?"

I ignore the heat rising up my neck and steady my breath. "The *Chasse*. It's supposed to be a gliding step where one foot chases the other."

Now, his lips graze my temple. "Is the *chasse* supposed to look like a herd of ponies in tutus galloping about?"

"Absolutely."

Then, his voice lowers to a smoking-hot growl. "We need to talk. Privately."

I bite my bottom lip as vivid pornographic images of us flash through my thoughts. I'm pretty sure if the man read the dictionary in that tone, he'd have half the women in Chicago dropping to their knees for him.

Even me.

I cross my arms, covering the goosebumps scattering up them, and redirect his attention to the girls clambering for his attention. "They're doing this for you, you know. Showing off."

His finger draws a soft line from my neck down my spine. "Is that why you're wearing this? To get my attention?"

"No," I snap aloud. So loud that all the girls stop and look up at us. "Perhaps you should go," I suggest. "We can talk later."

"We can talk now." Brash as all day, Enzo pulls out a wad of cash and fans it. "Twenty bucks to every girl who lines up in sixty seconds to go play with Mrs. Weston," he declares.

The girls squeal with excitement, forming a neat row. Enzo tosses the wad out the door, and twenty-dollar bills flutter like confetti.

"What are you doing?" I ask, puzzled.

"Giving us privacy," he replies. "Play with them," he orders to Mrs. Weston across the hall as if he owns the place.

And, for all I know, he does because nervously, she nods. Her pasted-on smile is so wide I'm genuinely worried she might be drunk.

Before he closes the door, with the smallest semblance of authority, I yell after the girls, "Only take one each."

Okay, that sounded weird, right?

Enzo shuts the door behind him and turns the lock, the sound echoing in the small room, making my heart race. His presence fills the space, and it feels suffocatingly small.

And when he takes a step closer and gazes down at me like that—like a man escaping a year in the desert, welcomed by a scotch over ice—I can't breathe.

We stare at each other for a long minute, as invisible, unspoken words swirl all around us.

Then, with a heavy sigh, his face falls as he says whatever he's come here to say. "I came to say goodbye."

CHAPTER 11
Kennedy

D<small>ID</small> he just say he's saying . . . *goodbye?*

What in the actual fuck?

My heart pinches, but I can't make a scene. And goddamnit, I will not cry. "Oh," I manage to say, trying to conceal just how deflated I feel inside. And I don't know why I can't just shut my mouth at a moment like this, but I add, "Will I see you again?"

"I doubt it," he replies, emotionless.

Meanwhile, I'm gutted from the inside out.

The longer I gaze at him, the more the desire to be closer to him intensifies. So much so that without permission, I tenderly caress his cheek.

"Look," he starts, interrupting the moment. "The debt you owe my uncle—"

"Is about to be paid off, thanks to you," I cut in, bubbling over with gratitude. "I owe you my life."

"No, you don't."

What's he going on about? Of course, I do. "I barely scraped together twenty grand."

"More like ten," he corrects me flatly, raising that impeccable eyebrow of his.

Emotions overwhelm me, and I hastily blink back a tear, cutting him off. "The point is, you were the only one who gave a damn whether I lived or died. And even if this whole mess ended up far, far worse, the fact that you did that means something. And *you* mean something. To *me*."

We linger in silence for a beat, his golden eyes locked on mine. Before it gets awkward, I speak up. "Promise me one thing?"

"Anything."

"You're not made of stone, Enzo," I murmur, smoothing my fingers along the bruises on his cheeks and jawline, then rising to my tiptoes to press a kiss there. "Take care of yourself." Then, I add, "*Lang may yer lum reek.*"

He draws back slightly. "What did you say?"

"Just something my dad used to say to avoid a lengthy goodbye. Technically, I think it means, *Long may your chimney smoke.*"

"I know what it means," Enzo replies, and the small crack in my heart widens even more. A man who knows Scottish. My dad would've loved him.

His gaze remains averted. Annoyed, he mutters, "I'm trying to say goodbye here, *Bella* . . . and you're giving me the equivalent of *Live long and prosper*?"

The quote from Star Trek makes me laugh, though I fight back more tears. *Da* loved that, too. "I guess so."

When his gaze meets mine again, he simply notes, "You're

crying." Mr. Obvious's words come out devoid of empathy and more like a statement of fact than anything else. As if there's no room in his world for emotions or outbursts.

Or me.

Still, it stings. I know Enzo D'Angelo is a rich, powerful mob boss, but it's as if I never mattered at all, and the connection we had was all in my head.

God, was it?

But . . . Wait a minute. If it was all in my head, then what's he doing here, breathing his fiery, cigar-scented Enzo hotness all over me like a dragon in heat?

I shake it off.

Nevermind. It doesn't matter.

Taking a brave step back, I inhale deeply, steel my emotions, and extend my hand. "I'll miss you, Enzo Ares D'Angelo."

He slips his firm grip through mine. "Goodbye, Kennedy Luciano."

The name Luciano grates on me the way it always does, and I want to correct him and tell him I prefer to go by Mullvain, but why bother? I'm never going to see him again.

For a long, tenuous beat, we stare. Then, just as I think he's about to turn and walk away forever, without warning, he kisses me.

And not some *last call*, goodbye forever, sweet farewell kiss. *Nooo.*

We kiss like every nuke on the planet has just been launched. In a rush, his lips crash against mine. And Enzo takes everything—*everything*—kissing me, breathing me in, consuming me so fully I see stars.

We melt into each other, tongues colliding, his arms so tight around me, there's no escape. Not that I would want to.

Gasping for air, we break apart only to crash together once more, the intensity of our connection igniting like wildfire between us.

The earth tilts as I'm lifted in the air, my body sprawled on a desk that's so rickety, I'm pretty sure it'll shatter if he tries to fuck me on it.

"We can't," I huff, panting and coming back to reality. "We're in a classroom," I pant. "With a bunch of kids right outside that door."

And you're leaving.

He rips off his tie, nostrils flared, completely out of control. "We're doing this. Now."

He's halfway through undoing his belt when I prop up on my elbows, and repeat myself. Albeit, less convincing. "We can't."

Two hands grip my knees and spread my legs. "The hell we can't."

Out of nowhere, the blare of a horn shatters the moment. Then it does it again and again, honking and sounding the alarm.

His gaze darts from me to the window, then down to the street below. "Shit," he mutters under his breath before bolting out the door.

I look outside to see what's going on. My eyes widen at the sight of three little girls climbing all over the hood of a very expensive sports car like it's the best thing in the world.

Enzo is a mob kingpin. With a gun. Headed right to three little ballerinas threatening to cave in the hood of his car.

Shit is right.

CHAPTER 12
Kennedy

PANICKED, I chase after Enzo, his strides threatening to unleash a Mach-4 storm on three very naughty little girls.

Once outside, he halts abruptly. I collide into him from behind.

"Hey!" he barks, attempting to sound every inch of the stern kingpin that he is. With both hands on his hips, he demands, "What do you zoo animals think you're doing?"

The girls, no taller than my waist and completely unfazed by his presence, laugh even louder as they slide down the windshield of the sleek, black sports car.

Assertively, he demand, "Get down from there this instant, or so help me . . ." He doesn't finish the threat. Instead, he lets the implications hang heavy in the air the way all parents do when they have no idea what to say next.

I can't help but wonder if he speaks to everyone like this—little children and dangerous thugs alike.

The girls continue treating his car like their personal jungle gym, giggling hysterically as they slide down the windshield and bounce on the hood.

He holds up a finger. "I'm going to count to three. One." Pause for effect. "Two." A second finger goes in the air.

Thankfully, before he can reach the dreaded *three*, they're all on the ground, front and center.

One of them, a curly-haired brunette with pigtails, points an accusatory finger at her friends. "It was their idea!"

His stern brow turns to me. "Are you going to tell her, or should I?"

"Tell her what?"

"Snitches get stitches."

Playfully, I smack him in the chest and pray he isn't serious. "They're very comfortable around you," I reply softly, hoping he somehow understands what a great day this is for them. "They're not like this with everyone," I add, hoping to butter him up.

"You're the only one I want comfortable around me."

When his car alarm goes off again, he rolls his eyes. "Stop leaning on the car."

The girls stand back up.

With a huff, he clicks his fob, stopping the noise, mid-honk. "You can't just climb all over someone's car like that. Do you have any idea how much a brand-new Aston Martin costs?"

The littlest one shrugs her shoulders. "A hundred dollars?" I bite back a smile as she hands him something. "Here you go, Zo." I'm momentarily stunned that she knows his name. Or, I think she knows it.

She puts whatever it is in his hands, and it looks delicate, like angel wings. "What is it?" I ask, curious.

"The hood ornament off the car." His voice is low, dangerous.

Shit.

My horrified eyes meet his, and I can sense the impending eruption. I step between him and the girls. "I'll pay for it."

"With what, *Bella*? Monopoly money?" My breath catches as both his hands grip my waist. He lifts me up like a rag doll and sets me aside with unsettling ease.

Then his heated gaze locks on the girls as their guilty glances morph into puppy dog eyes. Oh, they're good.

The ringleader, Lola, steps forward. "Sorry, Zo," she says, her voice dripping with the saccharine sweetness of a seasoned pro. "We won't do it again."

"You better not," he warns.

"It's just that it looks like a castle," she says dreamily.

Unimpressed, he raises a brow. "Yes, and in the real world, castles don't come cheap. And climbing on them is a one-way ticket to broken bones."

I gasp, stunned. He wouldn't really hurt them, would he? I shoot him a panicked look as he reaches for a twig on the ground.

To my surprise, he lowers to a knee, addressing them all, face to face. "When my sister was younger, she thought our father's car was the world's greatest trampoline. Want to know what happened to her?"

Wide-eyed, they listen attentively. I'm on edge, unsure of where this is going.

I can't help but interrupt *Story Time with Enzo*. The last thing they need is some terrifying tale that keeps them up at night. "Um, Enzo, can I have a word?"

He continues, his voice ominous. "She broke her leg. *Crack!*" He breaks the stick in two for effect. They all jolt, and he goes all in, full storyteller mode. "And do you know what happens when little girls break their legs?"

On the edge of their seat, they all look back at him. "What?" one of them asks.

He leans in dramatically as he enunciates every word. "They. Can't. Dance."

With that, he stands back up and points a stern finger at each of their noses. "No more jumping on cars." He huffs, agitated.

They giggle.

"Besides, what if you fell into traffic? You'd be squashed." He makes a sound effect and bulges his eyes.

They laugh louder, their cherubic faces beaming. "Okay, Zo!" The man oozes so much *natural born parent*, it's all I can do not to swoon.

He reaches into his pocket, and with a click, the car's lights flash. "You want to play? Do it on the inside."

They cheer wildly as if they've just been let loose in a candy store as Enzo takes a seat on the steps, pulls out a cigar, and lights it.

"What are you doing?" I ask, because he has no idea how much peanut butter and jelly might still be under their fingernails.

He looks up at me through a veil of smoke, his expression deadpan. "Slowly descending into the depths of hell. What does it look like?"

"You can't just let them play in your car." I stare as six little hands smudge fingerprints all over every inch of glass.

"Well, it's either that or shoot them, and you seem to be attached," he quips, the corners of his lips quirking up in amusement. Taking a slow drag from his cigar, he shoots me a sidelong glance, his eyes smiling for the first time since he arrived. "Sit down, Kennedy."

It's the way he says my name. Like I'm some sort of challenge he's trying to overcome. "Polite pass."

He clears his throat, the sound deep and rich. "I wasn't asking."

When my feet still won't budge, his irritation melts. "Sit down, *Bella*."

I hate how much I love when he calls me that.

Then he sweetens the deal. He nods towards the car, where the girls are still bouncing around like it's an amusement park ride. "Hurry before you miss out on the best show in town."

My hesitation fades away. Fair play isn't in this man's vocabulary. Enzo knows exactly where to strike, aiming a cherub's arrow right at my vulnerable soft spot, hitting dead center.

Slowly, I sit beside him, and feel a little like a puppy being trained.

For a moment, we sit in silence. Then my nerves get the better of me and I speak. "You're good with kids."

"I had babysitting duty a lot with Trinity."

"Trinity?"

He nods. "My sister." He gestures his cigar toward the car. "They remind me of her," he remarks, settling a hand on my knee, the possession of his touch potent.

I'm pretty sure the book of Enzo isn't cracked open very often. My hand smoothes over his. "I'd love to hear about her."

He blows out a long strand of smoke. "Once, Trinity had

the brilliant idea to 'decorate' our dad's brand new Mercedes. Nothing says *Happy Birthday* like a bedazzled steering wheel and a fire-engine red nail-polish happy face on the dash."

My hand squeezes his. "Your father must have been furious."

He shakes his head. "My father had this remarkable way of not yelling. He just gave us that disappointed look. And made me clean it up, of course."

"Why you?" I ask, fascinated by a D'Angelo family story that seems so . . . normal.

"Because I was responsible for her. I'd give anything to have that time back." His lips tip down, the look in his eyes full of sadness and regret. "I'm still responsible for her."

I nod. "I get it. I'd do anything for Riley."

He withdraws his hand from mine, and it's as if he's suddenly partitioning parts of himself off. I feel all the walls go up between us, and all I want to do is tear them back down.

He leans back, losing himself in watching three little girls engrossed in pretending to drive around town. "The point is kids will be kids," he mutters with so much regret I know not to pry.

If this really is the last time we'll see each other, I don't want it to end like this. I try to lighten the mood. Gently, I elbow him in the ribs. "I'm surprised the Chicago *god of war* is this easy going under the circumstances."

A small smile lifts his lips, but he doesn't look at me. "You know my nickname. Finally got around to googling me?"

"I figured it was only fair, considering you seem to be stalking me."

"How else am I supposed to find out your preferences in porn?" He puffs a circle of smoke through the air.

I lower my voice. "What makes you think I watch porn?"

"Everyone watches porn." His smile is short-lived as two women rush up the street, frantic as they start calling for their daughters.

The girls quickly hop out.

I jump to my feet. "It's fine, Ms. Adams and Mrs. Lee. The girls were just playing." Calmly, I introduce Enzo. "This is—"

"We're so s-sorry, Mr. D'Angelo," Mrs. Lee stammers, huffing and hastily pulling little Annabelle's death grip away from the steering wheel. Once dislodged, she shields her protectively.

It's obvious they know who he is. It's painfully obvious that I'm the only person in Chicago who failed to recognize him on sight.

Meanwhile, Ms. Adams attempts to retrieve Mackenzie, who defiantly clings to Enzo's lower leg, refusing to let go. "I want to play with Zo!" she protests, her tiny fingers gripping him tightly.

Her mother, visibly mortified, apologizes profusely as she gently pries her daughter's hands from around his thick calves. "I am so sorry," she murmurs, her cheeks flushed with embarrassment.

"Try picking up your kids on time," he scolds with the gentleness of a grizzly bear. "This woman is not your babysitter."

These women are practically bowing as they depart, and it's irritating. "I'm happy to watch them after school."

His eyes, like molten gold, lock onto mine. "Do not push me, *Bella*."

"Then don't speak for me," I snap back, shaking my head. "You can't just boss people around like they work for you."

He gestures to the retreating women, rushing away, with their little girls in tow, as if being chased by a ravenous wolf. "Apparently, I can."

By the time Lola's mom arrives, Enzo is in rare form. She hurries, out of breath as Enzo shakes his head. "You again. What did I tell you about being late?"

Lola's mom gasps for breath, her excuses coming out in pants and puffs. "Sorry . . . late delivery . . . missed the bus . . ."

I quickly intervene. "Lola's mom is an OB nurse."

Her mom props Lola on her hip. "You know babies. They come when they come," she offers.

Lola proudly brandishes her discovery from Enzo's car. "Can I keep it?"

My eyes widen when I realize what she's holding. A shiny flask. One which she's waving around enough that we all hear the booze sloshing inside it.

Enzo puffs his cigar, smiling. "Finders keepers."

Lola's mom laughs nervously. "Give it back to the nice man," she pleads, still trying to pry the flask from Lola's tight, two-handed grip.

Oh, good. I'm not the only one who had no idea who he was.

With a puff of his cigar, Enzo holds out a fist. "I'll trade you the flask for what's in my hand."

"What is it?" Little Lola asks, still clutching the flask tight, as if keeping it is actually an option.

"There's only one way to find out." He wiggles his fist.

I chime in. "I wonder what it is?" I ask to entice her.

Slowly, suspiciously, she hands over the flask, her eyes narrowed in suspicion.

To my shock, he hands her the angel wing hood ornament from his Aston Martin. Her mother obviously has no idea what it is, but still instructs her daughter to thank the nice man.

"Thanks, Zo," Lola says, clasping the charm to her chest with a smile that could light up the room.

"We'd better go or we'll miss the bus," her mother says, bidding us all an awkward farewell as they take off down the street.

I notice the empty space where chrome angel wings should be. "You didn't have to do that. I could've grabbed some Gorilla Glue."

"You think I'd let you within a foot of this car with Gorilla Glue? Maybe there's a chewed up wad of gum lying around. Or, duct tape."

"Maybe," I tease. "You let three little girls wreak havoc on the interior."

"Now, I'd like a full-grown woman to wreak havoc in it." He puffs his cigar, motioning towards his car. "I have a proposition for you. Get in."

"That doesn't make me sound like a prostitute at all."

Riled up, he mutters, "My life would be so much easier if you were."

"What's that supposed to mean?"

He shakes his head. "Just get in." When I hesitate, he adds, "unless you'd rather go wait for the bus with Lola's mother. I believe the creep that loves drooling all over your legs is holding a seat for you."

Bleh. I shut my eyes. "How is it that you know about that bozo?"

He holds open the front passenger door for me. My heart kicks up to a million miles a minute.

"I don't want to do this," I blurt out.

"Do what?" he says. "Be specific."

"Be a conquest. Just one of a thousand one-night stands."

He drops the cigar and completely ignores me. "Get. In."

I knot my arms tight. Part of me wants what he's offering. The horny part. And the part that foolishly believes he actually wants more than *wham, bam, thank you, ma'am*.

But the other part of me—the smart one—knows the reality of this situation. He's leaving. He said so himself.

Then he offers me the one thing—the only thing—I can't refuse. "You want to see your sister, don't you?"

I do. He knows I do.

So, I get in, watching as he gets behind the wheel. His stoic features grimace the second he does. "This car needs a bleach bath."

He pulls into traffic and his jaw tenses as he heads north. "Where are we going?" I ask.

I know he's heard me, but he doesn't answer right away. It's like he's working something out in his mind, deep in thought.

I can only take the suspense for so long, especially as we turn down a familiar street. "Where are you taking me?"

With a long sigh and a hard right at the light, he finally replies. "Your place."

CHAPTER 13
Kennedy

My place.

After the shock wears off, his words stick to my brain like gum under a park bench. Why are we going to *my* place?

I mean, he's leaving. He said so himself. With his outside voice.

Plus, he's a super mega bazillionaire. Why can't we go to his place? Or, at least get a hotel?

I mean, my place is a mess. And not just the normal mess.

Because my dog has separation anxiety, my apartment resembles the aftermath of a twister straight out of *The Wizard of Oz*. Not that it's ever been neat as a pin. But now, whenever I'm gone, Truffles totally loses his shit and pretty much tears the place apart.

It wasn't a problem when Riley was around. Her school summoning her back to Italy for an academic emergency—something I've never heard of—was nothing short of a miracle.

She'd been too engrossed in packing to notice me at all, waltzing in, clad in nothing but Enzo's blazer and his brother's comically large spare sneakers. Thank God, because really, what could I say under the circumstances?

Late night.
Kidnapped by thugs.
Barely escaped with my life.
Rescued by a mob boss who likely shot my captors for the hell of it.
Let this be a cautionary tale about the perils of dancing for cash.

Knowing that Riley is safe and sound and over four thousand miles away is a relief, but it leaves me with the problem at hand: Truffles.

The no-kill shelter got back to me right away. They assured me that with love, patience, and a crate, his anxiety would eventually subside.

Do they have any idea how much a crate costs?

For twenty minutes, I've been so wrapped up in imagining Enzo's reaction to the chaos that is my apartment, I only just realized he hasn't once asked for directions.

Not only does Enzo know my address by heart, he seems perfectly at ease weaving in and out of traffic with his hand entwined with mine.

I decide to lay it all on the line and speak my mind. A terrible idea, I know. Yet the words just fly out. "You're awfully affectionate for a guy who's about to ditch me."

His thumb dusts my fingers, but he stays silent.

"Can't you get a booty call somewhere else?"

"You are not a booty call," he grumbles.

"Then what would you call it? Because I'm pretty sure *hit-it and quit-it* is one of the basic definitions of a booty call."

The tires squeal to a stop in front of my place, as if the universe knew he was coming and left him a spot.

He gets out, rounds the car in a huff, helps me out, and leads me up. "I said you're not a booty call," he says under his breath.

"Liar."

We make our way through the building until we get to my door. Standing there, nerves fluttering, we both stare at it. Then, out of nowhere, Enzo D'Angelo, kingpin supreme and notorious womanizer, comes completely unhinged. "Keys!"

It's as if the very fabric of his being will combust if we don't have sex right here, right now. God, I'm so tempted to see what happens if I make him wait.

His expression turns desperate. "Kennedy," he warns.

I roll my eyes. "Okay, okay. But don't say I didn't warn you."

"Warn me about what?" Enzo asks as I twist the key in the lock. Suddenly, a furry ball darts out from behind the door, circling our feet. "What the hell?" he says, eyeing Truffles with a mix of confusion and disdain. "You own a . . . rat?"

I bristle at his comment. "He's a dog."

Enzo arches an incredulous brow. "Sure, he is." Truffles launches himself at Enzo's gazillion-dollar loafers with a friendliness that takes me by surprise. My heart leaps into my throat as I watch my tiny furball of a dog nip at his laces.

Enzo's reaction is swift, and I can feel my blood pressure spiking as he swoops in to scoop up Truffles, examining him closely. Panic courses through me, but before I can voice any protest, Enzo raises Truffles up to his face.

"Protecting your mom, are you?" he asks, his voice surprisingly gentle as he looks into Truffles's eyes.

Truffles plants a single wet lick on Enzo's nose, his tiny tongue leaving a trail behind. It softens the hard edges of Enzo's features, surprising me.

"Yeah, I guess he is," I admit, unable to conceal the warmth in my voice as I reach out to reclaim Truffles from Enzo's hands. "He saved my life," I say, meeting Enzo's gaze as he turns to face me.

Enzo looks down his nose at Truffles, his expression unreadable. "That makes two of us."

But he doesn't hand him over. Instead, he continues to stroke Truffles' fur, his gaze sweeping over my tiny apartment until it settles on the bed.

The bed is small, almost dollhouse-sized, next to his towering frame. His gaze shifts to the sofa, a worn-out piece of furniture missing a cushion.

Frowning, he strides over to the closet. If he thinks that cramped phone booth of a space is going to cut it, he's wasting his time.

At this point, I'm not even sure what to say, but the silence is unnerving. It's as if Enzo is just now processing how staggeringly different our stations really are and figuring out how to bow out of this *it's not a booty call* gracefully.

Then he opens a drawer—my *underwear* drawer—and I die on the spot. It's filled with undies of all vintages. You know—old, worn, elastic shot all to hell and back again.

With a single finger, he plucks out a pair of my panties. The black lace, pristine and untouched pair that has never seen the light of day. Mostly because I got them as one of those *open a line of credit and get a free pair* deals at a fancy boutique, but I've never had an occasion fancy enough to warrant them.

"This one," he declares.

My heart skips a beat. "This one . . . what?"

"*This one* is what I want you to wear. However, don't get too attached. I'll be ripping them from your skin and tasting your sweet, juicy cunt soon enough."

A small squeak escapes my throat. Wide-eyed, mouth agape, I just stare. He did not just say that.

With a wave of his hand, he continues, "And the blue dress in your closet," like he's ticking off items on a grocery list.

Stunned and confused, I finally manage to speak. "You want a fashion show?"

"I want you to pack a bag," he says, his tone leaving no room for argument.

"Pack? And where exactly am I going?"

Without missing a beat, he stretches a hand to the highest shelf in the closet—the one I need a chair for—effortlessly reaching for the duffle on the top shelf. It lands at my feet with a thud.

"Leaving town," he announces. His gaze meets mine as that signature, panty-melting Enzo D'Angelo smile finally takes form. "We're going to Italy."

CHAPTER 14
Enzo

"I am not going to Italy," Kennedy argues, though rather unconvincingly. "I can't."

This time, it's her bra drawer I rummage through. I pull out the black lace number with the tags still intact and toss it to her. "Why not?"

"Why not?" she echoes, dropping the bra into the bag like a good girl despite her protests. "Because I have to work."

"From what I hear, you're down to just the one job."

"How do you know that?"

I brush off her question, keeping my focus on the point I want to make. If only she knew how much I stalked her. "You've been working yourself to the bone," I assert, my tone matter-of-fact.

She nibbles that plump lower lip like she's mulling it over, and I know I've almost got her.

"What you need is a vacation," I counter, sidestepping the fact that her debt is no where near being paid, with Uncle Andre being the asshole he is.

It's pointless, so delving into all those details when working herself around the clock won't get her any less killed.

What she needs is an escape.

And what I need is to fuck this girl out of my system once and for all before I have to hand her over to Uncle Andre.

True, I'll be rushed, but a week should do it.

I picture her in nothing but the black bra and panties, on her knees, her big brown eyes staring up at me as I fist her hair and slide my thick cock between her full lips and down her throat.

The thought of Kennedy on all fours is glorious—and abruptly shattered as Rocco comes into view behind her. *"I'm gonna have a great time teaching your little pet how to take it in the ass for me."*

All of a sudden, Rocco and I are struggling over Kennedy like she's a goddamned wishbone when, out of nowhere, a low growl rips through my chest.

Followed by a *Ruff!*

The little dog barks, jolting me back to reality and intensifying the pain throbbing in the center of my head.

I pet his head and refocus on Kennedy. Her soft voice is uttering something adorably predictable and inconsequential. "I still have to teach," she says.

"I'm sure the owner will figure something out," I say, my tone brisk and authoritative. But her persistent pout softens my demeanor. "It's only for a week. She can manage without you for that long," I insist, though, after having met her, I have my doubts.

Kennedy remains resolute. "I need to give her notice."

"You need to pack, *Bella*. Now." I hold up the little dog to her face. "I'm taking a hostage until you're done."

She makes a grab for the dog, which is ridiculous. I simply hold him over my head, out of her reach.

"Give him back," Kennedy insists, bouncing up on her toes to try and reach Truffles with surprising determination.

"Pack," I counter firmly, my voice low as I glance at her bouncing breasts. I know it's a cheap thrill, but this woman has me wound up tighter than a drum with all this sexual tension.

A few months back, I would've had my fill—sated myself with supermodel sex fiends three at a time. But ever since this woman barged into my life, I swear, one look and she broke my dick.

The damn thing works for her and only her—totally fixated on her full lips and gorgeous, fuckable tits—and he hasn't even had her yet.

Goddamnit, I am fucking her to Milan and back again, and no one is stopping me.

Not even her.

Sadly, she gives up. "He's going to pee on your head."

What? Is that a thing?

AT THIS POINT, I DROP THE DOG AND BACK HER INTO a wall. "I said pack."

Her big eyes meet mine as she nibbles that lush, lower lip. "If I did go," she says meekly as if it's a choice, "could I visit my sister?"

Pressing my body against hers, I let the weight of my thick, angry, hard cock sink into that pretty head of hers. "You won't be in Italy for your sister, *Bella*. I'm not sharing you with your sister or anyone else. You'll be there for me." I fist her hair and steal access to her neck. I nip her ear and whisper, "And I'll be there for you. Only you."

"Just one week?" she breathes.

She smells like she smelled the other night—nothing special. Just a hint of cheap drug store soap and fear and *her*, and it's fucking addictive. "One week, Kennedy. And then I'll let you go."

For good.

Liar!

Shut up.

She swallows hard, her voice a raspy bundle of nerves. "And what do I get out of it?"

My eyes bulge. "An all-expenses-paid trip to Italy. Reprieve from this hellhole." Seriously, who needs convincing of this? Entire competitive game shows are built around it, for fuck's sake.

"And to be your living, breathing blow-up doll?"

"You make it sound like a bad thing."

The fire in her eyes is a wall of resistance that I either need to smother out or walk away from.

"Look around, *Bella*." She does. "What could possibly be holding you back?"

She thinks for a moment, and finally says, "You. You're holding me back."

CHAPTER 15
Enzo

Me?

I'm holding her back?

What in the actual fuck?

In disbelief, I shoot a glance down at the little dog at my feet. *Do you believe this shit?*

He returns a clueless stare.

My attention shifts back to the insane woman turning down a trip to Italy. "So, let me get this straight. You're rejecting a trip to Italy because of . . . me?"

Kennedy's stance is resolute, hands planted firmly on her hips as she speaks. "We both know that if you take me to Italy, *this*"—she gestures between us—"isn't exactly a PG arrangement."

I don't bother arguing back. The ringing in my ears has started up, signaling the onset of a jackhammer about to tear through my skull. Still, I hold my ground, silent but present, a lesson deeply ingrained within me by my mother.

Kennedy keeps going. "You're the kind of guy who gets his way and will want things from me..."

Her words drift as she thinks, nibbling her lip in that alluring way that manages to capture my attention despite the throb along my temples. "Things?" I ask, trying to sound thoughtful when I'm just trying to figure out what the fuck she's saying. "You mean sex?" I ask flatly.

In silent agreement, she nods, cautiously adding, "And I could get, well, hurt."

Hmm. I'm not sure if she needs a safe word or a limit list or what, but then it hits me. Eyes narrowed, my head tilts. "Are you a virgin?"

"No." The blush is so red, I wonder if she's lying. Not that it matters. I'll find out soon enough. Yet beyond my control, out of my mouth flies, "You're not my prisoner, *Bella*. You're my guest. You can leave at any time. Now pack."

Kennedy doesn't back down. "If I'm going, which is still a big 'if,' by the way, then I want something in return." She folds her arms, a move that would typically captivate me, but right now, the vise grip on my head is strangling my libido.

I rub my temples, trying to push back the pain. "Fine. Name it."

"No sex."

"What?" I snap, because the hell that's happening.

I think real fucking hard because the entire point of whisking Kennedy away to Italy is to bang her senseless. Not frolic around the Italian countryside, hand in hand, lazily reading cozy romances to each other.

Then, almost timidly, she adds, "I mean, no sex . . . not unless I see Riley."

"Riley." I know all about her—the sister. The one I've secretly hidden halfway around the world under the guise of a full ride scholarship program. Not that I have an altruistic bone in my body. I just needed her safely out of the way.

I figured Italy was far enough. My mistake.

"For every day I'm your '*guest*'"—she air quotes—"I'll be taken to and returned from Riley's place. I will spend a full three hours of uninterrupted time with my sister. Any time, day or night."

I smirk. Her little request isn't without risks, but it makes me grin all the same. "Considering I plan to wreck that pretty pussy of yours several times a day, *Bella*, what do you suggest? Shall I move her in? Perhaps pour her a drink, offer her a chair to make herself comfortable, and let her watch?"

She narrows her eyes. I narrow mine back. The air between us is damned near combustible.

"Three hours a day," she bargains, braver out of the silence. "Take it or leave it."

No one speaks to me like this. Ever. Because if they did, I'd end them. For a beat, I study her, intrigued. Someone didn't get the memo.

A low, satisfied growl emerges from my chest, and I'm not sure who's more surprised: her or me. Despite the deepening furrow across her brow, and delicate hands that suddenly aren't sure where to go, she straightens, pouting those gorgeous lips against a defiant chin.

What did it take for her to demand this? Kennedy is telling me exactly what she wants—what she needs—and I fucking relish it.

"Is that it?" I ask.

Her fingers weave through several strands of hair, a feeble attempt at smoothing them over a faded scar near her left brow. She's done this before. Tried, and failed, to cover her flaws.

Because she's stupid enough not to know that I see everything. All of her.

From the heart-shaped freckle on her neck to the nine scars lining her skin like a constellation—three on her face, four on her arms, a cigarette burn on her wrist, and another on her leg.

And it's all I can do not to kiss, lick, and worship every last one of them along with the rest of her body.

The one on her thigh is smudged enough that I know she fought—and that she was probably bound when it happened. It's faded enough that she had to be young. The one I can't wait to carve from her mind first.

I also want to know who did this to her—whether it's one man or more—mostly so I can string them up by their balls as I burn their fucking world to the ground, but that can wait.

"Yes," she replies, raspy as her big doe eyes meet mine. Fear and pain fade behind a storm cloud of want and need.

I let out a slow, smooth breath. "Fine," I say.

"Fine?" I see the shadows of doubt cross her expression, and know she still needs some convincing.

I step into her space until our bodies are almost touching, my hands safely tucked away in my pockets as my rock hard dick butts against the plane of her stomach. "I'm not about to force myself on you, Kennedy. And the only way you're getting any part of my dick is if you beg for it."

Finally, the tiniest smile emerges from her lips.

The curiosity in her big brown eyes and the blush creeping up her skins tell me she's in, but I need to hear her say it. "Tell me, here and now, you agree. Anything I want. Any way I want it. For the entire week."

"Anything?" She swallows loudly, and I imagine myself pumping down her throat.

"Anything," I demand low, brushing my lips against hers, sending a shiver across her body. Then deliberately, I step back, breaking the closeness between us. "Do we have a deal?"

Her staggered breath eases to a sigh as she nods. "Yes, Mr. D'Angelo. We have a deal."

Fucking finally. I lift her defiant chin, capturing her lips in a possessive kiss before gripping her hair firmly, eliciting a gasp from her. With deliberate force, I brush my lips against the scar she attempted to conceal. "Pack. Now. You have ten minutes."

Obediently, she nods, and I release her, watching as she hurries into her closet, away and out of sight. And the minute she does, a surge of pain crashes into my skull, intensifying tenfold from its initial hold.

I stumble back. *Fuck.* I focus on my breath, trying to steady myself.

Retrieving my flask, I sip. If I were into meds—legitimate ones, not the recreational stuff—I'd be floating on cloud nine. But ever since Trinity's attack and the issues with Smoke, the thought of swallowing a pill churns my stomach.

I rub the back of my neck, silently pleading with the pain gods for relief, when suddenly, the little dog at my feet goes ballistic.

Ruff!

His barking reaches a piercing pitch, and I entertain the idea of tossing him out the window to quiet him down. But I'm pretty sure my little deal with *Bella* hinges on me not murdering her precious dog, so that's out.

Like a lunatic, he begins leaping up my leg. I glare down angrily. "Do not hump my leg."

Ruff! Ruff-ruff!

To silence his incessant yapping and prevent any jizz on my slacks, I scoop the little bastard up.

Instantly, he settles, which is suspicious. Like the little bastard is plotting a sneak attack behind those innocent black eyes.

And just as I start to let my guard down, the dog springs up, his tongue darting over every inch of my face like it's drenched in steak sauce.

Ugh.

His freaking aardvark tongue gets me right up my nose holes.

Blech. What the fuck, dog?

The mutt nearly slips from my grasp as I stagger backward, narrowly avoiding a collision with the dilapidated remains of what was once a sofa.

"Everything okay?" Kennedy calls out.

No. Everything's not okay. Fuzzball here cleared all the boogers from my nose, then decided to test my reflexes with an attempted suicide dive from my arms.

I set him down. "Everything's fine."

Fine, except for the pain radiating from the base of my head to the back of my eyes. Scanning my choices—the lumpy bed or the cushionless sofa—I opt for the bed, collapsing onto it with a heavy exhale.

I take a deep swig from my flask, hoping the Macallan will offer an ounce of relief.

A second later, the mutt hops onto the bed and makes his way to my chest, resting his face against it. His presence is oddly comforting. With my eyes firmly shut, I mutter, "Do not piss me off."

He responds with a sleepy yawn, and surprisingly, the urge to wring his neck never surfaces.

Instead, I find myself absentmindedly stroking his fur. The ball of fluff and his annoying snores settle against me tighter as my mind wanders aimlessly.

Maybe there's a dog pound between here and the airport.

Or, a taxidermist.

CHAPTER 16
Kennedy

INHALE.

Exhale.

Don't puke.

Here I am, sitting in a car probably worth more than my entire existence—Andre D'Angelo estimated my worth at a hundred grand—feeling like I'm about to lose my lunch. Truffles, my impromptu emotional support dog, is nestled sweetly on my lap as Enzo, my kingpin sex god, holds my hand.

I steal a glance at his ruggedly handsome face, all calm and broody, with chiseled cheeks and dark stubble. His golden eyes are glued to the road, probably imagining all the things he'll want me to do—anything he wants, any way he wants it.

Meanwhile, I'm here, feeling like I'm on a rollercoaster ride from hell, with my stomach doing somersaults and my lunch threatening to reappear.

It's not even the idea of going to Italy that has me unsettled, though it's not helping. Planes have never been my thing. Keep your flying superheroes: I'm Team Shifters. All day. Everyday.

No. What's got my nerves twisted like Christmas tree lights in a storage box is the fact that I'm flying halfway around the world, and for what?

To see Riley. But that's only for three hours a day.

The rest of the time, I'll be at the beck and call of big, bad Enzo D'Angelo. And why? So he can keep me naked and chained to a bed post, ravaging my body any way he wants?

And why does it feel like the heat kicked on?

My father's advice swims laps through my mind. *When life throws you curveballs, ya catch, darlin'.*

How the hell do I catch a curveball like Enzo D'Angelo? It's like trying to snag a shooting star—fast and fiery. He's uncatchable.

Absently, I scratch behind Truffles's velvety ear, seeking solace in his calm presence.

"What's wrong?" Enzo asks, his gaze fixed on the road ahead. He's been deep in thought the entire time, and neither of us has said a word. How he knows something is wrong is beyond me.

"What makes you think something's wrong?"

"Because if you rub that dog's ear any more, the damned thing will catch fire." His eyes flick to mine. "What?"

I let go of Truffles's soft ear and clasp my hands together, trying to sound composed despite the whirlwind of nerves inside me. "It's just that I—I've never left the country before. Don't I need a passport or something?"

"It's been taken care of," he says with that sense of authority that normally makes him totally hot. In this moment, hearing those words come out of his mouth is just . . . terrifying.

When I frown, he notices. How he notices, I have no idea

since he hasn't bothered looking my way since we got in the car. "What?" he prods.

I shake my head. "Nothing." I know, I know. It's a big, fat lie.

Which he must read all over my face. His hand reaches into his blazer and tugs a flask from his pocket. "Here." He hands it over. "This will help."

I shake it. Surprisingly, it's full. I caught glimpses of him swigging it while he was waiting. "I'm surprised there's anything left," I quip, unscrewing the cap and sniffing the contents before giving a long, leisurely inhale.

Mmm. Scotch. It reminds me of Da.

"Trust me, *Bella*, when it comes to me, you'll always have more to take," he retorts, his words decidedly naughty.

My legs clench in response, and the squeak that escapes my throat is audible as I take a swig, swallowing the smooth burn. The drink coats my throat, melting into my insides until most of my nerves wash away.

When we reach a checkpoint, an intimidating guard nods before waving the car through. Enzo pulls forward to a secluded area of the airport.

There, a private jet waits, flanked by a team of formidable security detail. They're good-looking, impeccably dressed, and armed to the hilt—a stark reminder of who Enzo D'Angelo is and that he's not to be fucked with.

I take another swig. "Thanks," I say meekly.

He studies me. "Note to self: this one drinks like a fish and needs her own flask."

This one. Two little words that instantly have me scowling, though, he's not wrong.

It's been years since I've had scotch, and the stuff was as smooth as kitty litter. But after *Da* passed, I'd do anything to get close to him. Sleep in his bed. Wear his T-shirts. Even drink stuff that would grow hair on my chest and easily pass for kerosene with just a hint of armpit sweat.

It took over a year to go through *Da's* last bottle. But by the last drop, I'd acquired the taste.

As my hand reaches for the door handle, it swings open, and I get a full frontal of the enormous beast before me.

It's big. It's black. And it's got DEATH TO ALL WHO ENTER written all over it.

It's a jet. *His* jet. With a giant capital D on the tail, which I assume stands for *D'Angelo* and not *dick*.

My heart stops, and I freeze.

Gently, Enzo's hand takes mine. "Don't worry, *Bella*. There's more booze on the plane."

"Har."

He ushers me across a black carpet to the stairs. Amidst the intimidating figures standing guard is a woman. A very beautiful woman with chestnut brown hair, a bright pink suit, and a vibrant red scarf. Somehow, she seems familiar.

She's sporting just enough cleavage to make me wonder if Enzo is looking for a threesome.

Because, shit, what if he is? I mean, my deal with the devil didn't even have fine print. It was exceptionally clear: *anything*.

I swallow hard, not sure I could actually munch on a taco. *Could I?*

Her warm smile widens as her glittering eyes glaze over my body as I down the rest of the flask.

"You must be Ms. Luciano," she greets me, her tone polite.

Professional, even. Her use of Jimmy's last name doesn't irritate me nearly as much as the alcohol works its way through my veins.

"Kennedy," I say, breathier than intended. Partially because of the booze, but more because Enzo just slipped his warm hand onto the small of my back.

"And this must be Ruffles," she coos, reaching for the dog in my arms.

"Truffles." At least one of us should have our name right.

"Savannah Whitaker," she says, extending a hand with a warm smile. Recognition dawns.

She's famous. Like, has her own show and brand of organic dog food kind of famous. The go-to person for celebrities—as in *Dog Trainer to the Stars* Savannah Whitaker.

My heart races with worry. Why is she here? Is she taking Truffles away?

"He'll need a quick walk before our flight," she reassures me, her voice soothing as the words *our flight* settle in. Before I can react, a bedazzled leash is wrapped around my little dog's tiny neck, and off they go.

He looks ridiculous. And adorable. Prancing about like some high-priced show dog strutting his stuff for a competition. It's as if he knows how impressive Savannah Whitaker is.

Her happy-go-lucky giggles encourage the little guy, and it tugs at my heartstrings, watching my little dumpster buddy experience the life he deserves.

They walk further away, and a trace of unease lingers in the air. "She's joining us?" I ask.

Enzo, absorbed in texting, nods without looking up. "Yes," he confirms, his thumbs tapping away. Then he adds, "It's a ten-hour flight. I want you all to myself, *Bella*. If you're preoccupied with the dog, you won't be able to focus."

"Focus?"

"On me."

I gaze up at him, stunned. "You hired a celebrity dog trainer just so I can spend the better part of ten hours tending to your needs?"

Finally, he pockets his phone and lets out a slow breath. He takes two steps closer, his presence commanding, his gaze intense. "No, *Bella*," he murmurs, his eyes darkening. "So I can tend to yours."

Holy fuck.

He wants to tend to my needs? Because of all the men I've been with, which I could count on one hand, not one of them was interested in tending to my needs. Hell, my needs were better satisfied with a hot novel and my hand.

Unexpectedly, he cradles both my cheeks in his hands, and the temperature jumps a hundred degrees. His kiss is smooth and hard and so unapologetic. Instantly, my panties are soaked.

When his tongue swipes through my open lips, I can't breathe.

All I can think of is the way his stubble would feel between my legs. His kiss deepens, and—did I say a hundred degrees? Make that a thousand degrees.

His arms wrap around me, and my body is forced forward onto his cock, and there's a whole lot of it. So much, in fact, my gasp is audible.

I'm a little stunned.

And scared.

It's been a long time for me and, oh, hell, am I even going to be able to stand by the end of this flight?

Ruff-ruff!

His lips tear from mine as we turn to see Truffles prancing around like it's the best day ever. "I can't believe you arranged this for him," I say, genuinely surprised he didn't shoot little Truffles and toss him on the grill.

"I did this for me," he says, tightening his hold around my waist. "Cute and cuddly is the worst cock block ever."

A light laugh bubbles up from my chest as he kisses my temple tenderly, and for a moment, everything feels so right. In a surreal, twilight zone sort of way. What's happening here? Do all mafia men have a need to play house?

Or just Enzo?

And is that what we're doing? Playing?

Not that I'm complaining. If anyone needs an escape from reality, it's this girl.

Enzo's gaze remains fixed on Savannah as she effortlessly commands Truffles to sit and stay, a task the little dog surprisingly masters in an instant. Meanwhile, I keep stealing glances at him.

His rugged features, softened by the gentle curve of his full lips and thick brows, make him undeniably gorgeous. But beneath that exterior lies an arrogant and dangerous man, legendary for leaving broken bones and shattered hearts in his wake.

We're interrupted by one of his men, and instantly, Enzo snaps our connection apart. Though I can't hear what the guard is saying, I can tell by the shift in Enzo's expression—

SINS & LIES

from easy-going to hardened stone—whatever he's saying isn't good.

"Get on the damn plane," he orders sharply, his voice leaving no room for negotiation.

"What's going on?" I press, my heart thudding hard against the cage of my ribs. Is it Uncle Andre? Or Rocco? Or any number of other threats this man probably deals with every hour, on the hour?

But he doesn't respond, his attention focused elsewhere as he adjusts his lapel with precision.

"Enzo, what's going on?" I repeat, pressing for answers.

Ignoring my plea, Enzo snaps his fingers.

What the fuck? Did he just snap to shut me up?

I open my mouth, ready to give him a piece of my mind, when a guard swoops in, tosses me over his shoulders like a sack of rice, and hauls me to the plane. "Hey!"

Truffles and Savannah are swallowed in the bodyguard's wake, following obediently, as if this bizarre scenario is completely normal.

Once up the stairs and inside the cabin, the guard gently sets me on my feet. "Apologies, ma'am," he says before swiftly pointing a finger in warning. "Don't get off the plane." With that, he exits.

Savannah settles in with Truffles while a flight attendant magically appears, offering champagne. Which only confirms my suspicions: I'm the only sane one here.

Savannah takes the flute, kicks off her shoes, and takes a sip, all casual-like, while I stand there, dumbfounded. "What?" she asks with a shrug. "You know how it is. Boys will be boys."

Boys will be boys? Is that what they call it when Scarface decides to make a cameo and riddles the plane with bullets?

Right. Drink up, crazy lady. Drink up.

I glue my gaze out the window as my blood runs cold. A sleek black car with blackout tint zooms past every last member of Enzo's security detail and screeches to a halt.

A hulking figure emerges. With a surly expression, muscles straining against his shirt, and dark shades that scream tough guy meets runway model, I'm not sure what to think.

From the looks of him—tall, dark, and menacing—I have a pretty good idea who he is.

And me being here? It's not good.

Not good at all.

CHAPTER 17
Enzo

I STRAIGHTEN my cuff as the black car races toward me at record speed. One look at the driver, and I brace for impact.

The sleek sports car screeches to a stop. Wisely, my men maintain their distance. They've been with me long enough to know better than to interfere.

Hmm. He's wearing my sunglasses. Which means he's been snooping through my shit again. I wonder what else he stole.

Dante advances like an impending storm, his strides deliberate, his presence pure *don't fuck with me*.

It's a sight to behold, watching my usually composed and collected brother lose his absolute shit. Like having a seat, front-row, center, at the eruption of Mt. Vesuvius.

He grabs me by the shirt with a grip that could crush steel. "What the hell, Enzo?" His voice is a low growl, the anger barely contained.

I can't help but flash him an innocent smile. "Problem, Dante?"

His eyes practically shoot fire as he gestures angrily towards the shiny new jet behind us. "Do you want to tell me why my black card has been charged for a fucking jet?"

I shrug, admiring it. "I needed a plane," I reply casually.

Dante waves a hand towards the jet. "Obviously," he mutters, his tone dripping with sarcasm.

"Besides, doesn't it feel good to get all that pent-up frustration out? You need this kind of release. God knows you're not getting it through sex."

He pinches the bridge of his nose. "What's wrong with your plane? And do not lie." He gives me that frustrated look that means a punch might be headed for my throat.

So, I explain. "Between the media and Uncle Andre, I'm constantly tracked by bloodhounds. I needed my space. My privacy."

"You need a swift kick to the ass, that's what you need." Dante takes a breath, looks skeptically at the plane, then back at me. "Privacy," he repeats slowly. "For what?"

Uh-oh.

This is the problem with having brothers. Crack open the door even a smidge, and they'll bulldoze right through. Nosy as all hell and always up in my business.

And do I spill about Kennedy?

Not even if every last one of my fingernails was being ripped from the skin. Dante would never let it go. He'd launch into endless lectures about having a conscience and respecting women, yada, yada, yada...

But because Dante runs ten miles every damn day, he zips past me like a gazelle before I can stop him.

I scurry after him, practically crashing into him as soon as we're inside the doors.

SINS & LIES

"Hello," Savannah says, all flirty smiles when she sees Dante.

Confused, he waves back. "Uh, hello." His gaze flicks between her and the dog, then he shoves me back and whispers, "You're seeing Savannah Whitaker, '*Dog Trainer to the Stars*'?" He air quotes for effect.

He knows damn well she's not my type. At all. I make sure we're out of earshot. "I am not dating Savannah Whitaker," I scoff under my breath. Not in a million years.

She's like a bone china doll—beautiful and polished but utterly pretentious and high maintenance. The kind of woman who's obsessed with taking selfies and a nightmare to fuck.

"Then what's she doing here?" Dante asks.

I glance at her and try to think. "She's . . . training my dog."

"You have a dog?" Horrified, he looks back at the useless ball of fur. "Does the ASPCA know about this?"

I sock him in the chest. "You know I've always wanted a dog."

"When you were eight." We both look on as Savannah takes a selfie with the little guy. Dante turns back, skeptical. "I'm not buying it. You didn't buy a jet to take a dog to Italy."

"You're right. I didn't buy the jet. You did." This time, it's him who socks me in the chest. *Ow*.

Then he sniffs the air. "What is that?"

The issue is, I smell it too. Floral with that alluring hint of lemon that follows Kennedy wherever she goes. I try to throw him off. "Jet fuel," I state.

"It's not jet fuel, it's not her," He points to Savannah as he steps towards her. "And it's definitely not him." He points to the panting patch of fur on Savannah's lap. "There's someone else here. I can smell her."

Dante heads for the back room as Savannah chugs her drink and tries not to pay attention.

I grab his arm. "First of all," I point out, "you saying that is just creepy. No wonder you don't have a woman. Your vibe is too Hannibal Lecter. And second, there's no one else here. You're simply starting to crack." I throw an arm around his shoulder and try to lead him out. "There's an excellent shrink I could recommend."

"I bet you could." Dante weasels out of my arm and rushes for the back. He throws open the doors and puts both hands on his waist.

Protectively, I rush in. If by some miracle Kennedy decided to get with the program—lying buck naked with those sculpted, soft thighs spread in the center of my bed—no one sees her but me.

But no such luck.

"What the fuck?" he asks.

And *what the fuck* is right.

Front and center on the bed are an assortment of toys. Dog toys. Along with treats. And outfits. So many fucking outfits it's like the damned dog is having a baby shower. Or he's one of those bears you stuff at the mall. What are they called again?

Dante picks up one of the outfits, still on a little hanger with one finger. "Are you fucking kidding me right now?" He roars with laughter and makes a call on his phone.

And this is where I can feel the tip of the cock, pushed in an inch and ready to fuck me up the ass—without lube—and there's not a goddamned thing I can do about it.

I am not telling them about Kennedy. Period. No matter how much I have to bite down and take it.

His phone rings out. Great. A FaceTime. A group one. With *all* of them. "Guess who's suddenly into this?" He holds the tiny outfit to the camera.

Their eyes light up as he dances it around the screen. "What the hell is it?" Dillon asks, smiling wide.

"Is he supposed to put that on his dick or something? Like some weird kink?" Mateo howls and waves a finger in my direction. "You are one sick shit."

"I second that." Smoke chuckles.

I snatch it from Dante's hand. "This is not some furry cock ring, you twisted shits. It's a . . ." I make a face. *What the hell is it?* I inspect the little leather jacket with a fur-lined collar and sleeves. It's like something you'd give a drag queen at a biker bar. If that drag queen was a squirrel.

Bzzz-bzzz.

A small noise comes from the closet. I'm not sure if Dante heard it, too, but as soon as he looks that direction, I blurt out, "Yes, I have a dog."

"One you're playing dress up with?" Dante says, grabbing another hanger. This one is purple with a frilly collar. All it's missing is heels and a powdered wig, and he'd be a dead ringer for Marie Antoinette. Or Elton John.

They all wait for my response. If I deny it, who knows when this torture will end. I take a breath. "I have a dog. It has clothes. Despite keeping my distance from everyone, I have a touchy-feely soft side. One that you fuckers wouldn't know anything about."

The room falls silent, a welcome reprieve. But, predictably, it doesn't last long.

Smoke's sharp gaze lands on me, suspicion evident in his

raised brow. "Getting a dog to connect with us?" His tone is laced with skepticism.

My internal alarm blares. *Abort mission.* But it's too late. I nod anyway.

He leans in closer to the screen, disbelief across every line of his face. "Then what's its name?"

Damnit. Smoke knows me too well. *Ruffles? Duffle?* No, think. Something edible. "Truffles," I say with confidence.

After a split second of silence, their laughter erupts even louder. It's all I can take. "Goodbye," I declare, ending the call abruptly and ushering Dante towards the door.

We pass Savannah, still seated and sipping like a camel. "Bye, Savannah. Bye, Truffles," Dante says, bidding them both farewell.

Truffles barks on cue, his timing impeccable. At least he's good for something.

We arrive at the steps. "Oh, and thanks," I add before Dante leaves, handing him the fob for his Aston Martin. I refrain from telling him that I've gifted the hood ornament to a little girl who will probably use it to pick her nose.

"If you so much as breathed on her wrong," he warns.

With a smirk, I pat him on the shoulder. "Not a scratch."

CHAPTER 18
Kennedy

HEART POUNDING, I see the fight breaking out between Enzo and a guy who looks so much like him, they have to be related.

Whatever's happening between them, I'm pretty sure he doesn't want me meeting anyone in his family.

And certainly not like this.

As his look-alike bolts up the stairs, two at a time, my heart beats so hard, that I feel it in my ears. I spring to my feet and dash past Savannah and Truffles, and bolt through the very last door at the back of the plane.

The one I assume is a bathroom.

The door clicks shut behind me, and my heart sinks as I realize this isn't the bathroom. Luxuriously furnished with six overstuffed pillows, a plush down comforter, and an obnoxiously oversized king-size bed that practically screams *big fucking deal*.

Oh, my God. I stare in horror because it's a bedroom.

It's *his* bedroom.

We're on a plane, right?

In the center of the bed sits a gift basket, practically begging to be investigated. I inch closer, my steps hesitant at first, then way too interested. My father used to say I had the curiosity of a cat.

Um, try a dozen.

The small, pink note attached reads,

To the best boy ever.
xo, S. W.

S. W.?

Savannah Whitaker. I'm not sure why I'm suddenly glaring at the card, but I am.

Is Savannah calling Enzo the best boy? Because that's just weird.

Nosily, I rummage through the gift basket. What exactly did Ms. Whitaker get *her best boy?* Because if it's chocolates, I'm eating them.

I don't know what I was thinking I'd find, but when I tug out an item that looks like a glittery jock strap, I snort. Out loud. Because . . . "What the hell?"

Then, I turn it upside down to find it's not a jock strap at all. It's a vest. A little sequin vest that's just big enough for Truffles. I stare at it and shake my head because it's adorable. A little over-the-top, but hell, the dog is in a private jet with a celebrity trainer. Maybe nothing is over the top.

Next, I find a ridiculously cute fur-lined leather jacket, and I'm starting to feel like next to my dog, I'm the underdressed one. Clearly, he now has a stylist. I scan the tag and gasp.

How is this puppy costume five hundred dollars? All the clothes in my closet combined aren't five hundred dollars. Is Idris Elba posing with him?

Because I could totally go for that.

I hold up the outfit and imagine Truffles prancing about in it at the dance studio, spreading joy to all who enter.

The little girls would go absolutely insane. Probably fight for who can behave the best for the sheer privilege of walking my little circus dog and picking up his poop.

Win-win.

Voices in the cabin snap me from my daydream. They're getting louder. I press an ear to the door, though I'm not sure why. They're loud. And headed this way. "There's someone else here. I can smell her."

Um, creepy.

What's worse than being caught on Enzo's plane? Being caught in his bedroom.

Panicked, I toss the outfit on the bed—no time to tidy up—and rush through the nearest door. Which seems to be to a closet.

As a matter of fact, it seems to be *my* closet. Except it's eight-thousand times bigger and smells fresh like a fancy hotel.

My beat-up duffle bag rests on the floor, surrounded by all my neatly hung clothes. There are three oval windows across the back, and *sheesh*, you could park a car in here.

Okay, maybe not a car, but at least a Harley.

A loud, "What the fuck?" has me nearly jumping out of my skin.

Enzo and presumably his brother are intense. And fun. So fun. When his brother calls the rest of them—and apparently, there are a lot of D'Angelo brothers—they're not the big, scary mob bosses from the headlines. They're playful and sweet, teasing each other and sharing jokes.

Mostly at Enzo's expense, which I have to cover my mouth not to laugh out loud at. Discovering that big, bad golden eyes will take *so* much shit from his brothers, it's endearing. It's like me with Riley—times five.

I'm hanging onto every word, but not so much that I can't multitask. I glance around. *Hmm.* Did they unpack everything? Several drawers catch my eye.

With silent, stealth-like moves, I slide open a drawer. My heart leaps into my throat, and my breath catches.

Three neat rows of my underwear greet me, alongside more neat rows of brand new, lacy ones with tags still intact. And, because Enzo is a guy, most of them appear to be thongs.

Has this man not seen my ass? It eats thongs for lunch.

Carefully, I lift a particularly pretty red pair. They're exquisite. See-through lace boy shorts in that dangerous combination of illicit *and* expensive. So expensive, I might need white gloves just to handle them.

I hold them against my body, realizing they're a perfect fit. Did he pick these out himself?

I set them down and pick up another pair. My mouth falls open as I discover this one—black and leather—also happen to be crotchless. In my pocket they go as I'll be flushing those down the toilet as soon as I get out of here.

Which brings up a good question: When you flush on a plane, where exactly does it go?

I picture some poor unsuspecting cow in a field, getting a

face full of blue liquid and pleather, and decide he or she cannot be victim to Enzo's depraved porn tastes.

I'll simply wait until we're somewhere over the ocean, I guess.

Ocean.

Nerves dance along my neck as I envision the plane ascending into the abyss of dark sky and sea. Refusing to succumb to the fear simmering beneath the surface, I move on to the next drawer.

I chuckle to myself as I sift through the drawer, finding a mishmash of bras, mostly new ones, thank God. Let's face it, my old bras have seen more wear and tear than a copy of *Fifty Shades of Grey*—library edition.

I pick one up and mold it against my girls. Another perfect fit.

How the hell does he know my size?

I catch a glance of myself in a full-length mirror, the cream lace trimmed with rose gold thread.

Don't know, don't care.

The crotchless panties might be a bust, but I'm definitely keeping these.

Finally, I get to the bottom drawer. As soon as I open it, my eyes snap wide as all the blood in my body rises in a hot flash up my cheeks.

It's long, it's pink, and absolutely nothing could mortify me more.

It's. A. Vibrator.

Correction: it's *my* vibrator.

And, yes, I may have thrown it into my bag because it was

already in my underwear drawer, and I had to make a split-second decision, not that I would necessarily need it.

I mean who am I kidding? This is Enzo *Fucking* D'Angelo, the man for whom there's a website dedicated to *that* as his middle name, along with the hashtag *KingpinSexGod*. It's like a fan page with hundreds of pictures of drop-dead gorgeous women dripping off his arms.

And yes, I checked him out. More like an investigative journalist and less like a stalker.

At least, that's what I keep telling myself.

These nut jobs actually have bets on which he's had more of: kills or lays.

And I just wasn't sure if he'd always be a *warm a girl up* kind of guy, or more rough and impatient and eager to cram every last inch of man meat in to the hilt.

And there's a whole lot of it to cram in. So much so, that I probably should've brought lube and a shoehorn.

I mean, yes, so maybe between those dangerous eyes and sinfully talented tongue, the man is a walking flame-thrower between the thighs. But it's a week.

A week!

And if the website is accurate, multiple times a day is part of the package, and vanilla isn't in his vocabulary.

I think of it. Seven whole days. Of him doing whatever the hell he wants, whenever the hell he wants. Nerves dance along my skin as tension wracks across me.

Bzzz.

Without warning, the damned thing goes off in my hand. It buzzes. Loud. *Argh!* I nearly drop it, twisting the stupid end of it. *Shut off, shut off, shut off!*

The room outside goes quiet. Too quiet.

The steady thump of dread fills my ears until I hear Enzo shout, "Yes, I have a dog."

After a tense moment of silence, the conversation continues, and I'm not sure, but it feels like Enzo's lying through his teeth to distract his brother. But when I hear him say, "*Despite keeping my distance from everyone, I have a touchy-feely soft side,*" my heart aches.

It takes a minute to process his words.

He's kept distant from his brothers. And it's so obvious he loves them—I mean, who would eat this much shit and keep asking for more? So, he's been keeping distant from his own family, just as I've been doing with mine.

Realization hits me square in the chest.

He's protecting them. He protects them the way I protect Riley. By staying away.

And from the sounds of it, it's killing him. Just as much as it kills me.

There's a long silence before the door opens in a rush.

Enzo looks down at me, his glance moving from me to the vibrator I'm still holding like an idiot. "*Bella*, if you started without me, there will be consequences," he rumbles, his tone bubbling over like hot-buttered sex.

There's so much electricity flowing between us it could light space. When he kisses me, I kiss him back. It's not timid or gentle. Not some shy wallflower kiss. It's hungry. Desperate.

Like for the first time in my life, I'm not thinking of anything or anyone else.

Or maybe I'm just not thinking.

And with his big, thick erection pressed hard against my belly, who could think?

Bump.

The floor moves from under us. My heart jumps against the wall of my chest. "What was that?"

"Us," Enzo growls. "About to tip the earth off its fucking axis."

CHAPTER 19
Kennedy

ENZO PULLS me into another toe-curling kiss when several knocks sound at the door.

"What?" he snaps.

The door creaks open, just a fraction, and the flight attendant keeps her eyes averted as she speaks. Like she's been in this position so many times, WHAT HAS BEEN SEEN CANNOT BE UNSEEN is written all over the poor woman's face. "Sorry, sir. We're about to take off."

He nods and leads me by the hand back into the main cabin, past Savannah and Truffles, guiding me to my seat. He plants another soft kiss on my lips, a lingering caress, as he clicks the belt around my waist. "Need more booze?" his raspy voice offers.

Shivering, I shake my head softly. "No, thanks."

He settles into the seat beside me, and I steal a glance back at Truffles. He's curled up under a plush Dalmatian print blanket, sound asleep.

Savannah's buried in her phone. Despite her prim posture

without a hair out of place, I'm betting she's knee-deep in Regency porn or something equally scandalous.

Suddenly, the room lurches, and I snap forward, gripping the armrests with white-knuckle force.

The next few bumps are jarring, each one sending a shiver down my spine. Then we really pick up speed.

I make the mistake of glancing out the window, and my heart lodges in my throat.

I hate this.

I hate that I'm ready to do anything. *Anything*. Beg if I have to. And not in a fun way. In the *I'm about to die* way. The next bump throws one word out of my throat. "Please!"

"Please?" Enzo replies, confused.

"Can we please drive?"

"To Italy?"

Okay, fine. I'm too delirious to know what I'm saying.

For a long beat, he studies me as frustration rolls off him in waves. Along with it, the sexual tension that's always brewing just below his surface.

His words come out stilted. "You've never flown?"

I shake my head. Another bump, and I cry out, latching on to his arm.

"And you're frightened?" he asks, his tone dark and amused. Because my claws digging into his skin aren't enough of a hint.

Petrified would be a better description. So much so that I'm borderline hyperventilating, trembling my way to a full-blown panic attack.

I manage to squeak out a small, "Yes."

The moment we ascend into the sky, he peels me away from his body with deliberate slowness.

Then, in one brisk move, the world tilts as he whisks me to the back of the plane and tosses me to the center of the bed.

Ah, yes. The bed.

Because that's how rich, powerful men roll. With a king-size bed tucked in the tail end of their flying death tube.

Swiftly, he positions himself over me, his knees locking me in place. Wide-eyed, I panic. "What are you doing?"

He tears off his tie and smiles as his gaze holds mine. "Showing you the only thing you need to fear, *Bella*, is me."

What? I open my mouth. To protest. To beg for mercy. The hell if I know. Squirming does nothing. I'm trapped beneath his weight.

Without warning, his massive hand locks around my throat, nearly cutting off my air.

Instincts surge through me like a raging river. My two small hands barely manage to wrap around his, my body thrashing as every part of me focuses solely on him.

The more I struggle, the tighter his grip, his darkening eyes fixed on mine.

Near tears and out of breath, my body gives up and I still.

His grip eases enough that I suck in a breath. "What the actual fu—"

"Are you wet, *Bella*?"

Wet? What? Why would I be . . .

Heat rushes up my neck—embarrassment blurring with shame—as I begin to register the thrum of arousal between my thighs.

I'm not just wet. I'm soaked.

"Answer me," he demands.

I squeeze shut my eyes. *So wet.* "No," I breathe.

A feral moan escapes his chest. "You'll pay for that lie, *Bella*." Slowly, he moves his body beside mine, but doesn't let go. With nothing but his iron grip around my neck, he's in total control.

Enzo's always in control.

"Who do you think you are?"

"You want to know who I am, *Bella*? I'm your greatest fear. Your worst nightmare. An untamed beast. The devil himself. And the only man who will ever fuck you again." His eyes darken. "Touch yourself."

He doesn't understand what he's asking of me. How could he? "I can't."

He doesn't ease up. With his other hand, he holds up the vibrator. Did I drop it on the bed? Tears prick at my eyes, burning a trail down my skin as he traces the toy along the swell of my breasts and down between my legs. "I said, touch yourself."

I can't do this. All I feel is Jimmy's disgusting hands between my legs. *It's either you or Riley, Kennedy.* Like it was my choice to let him fuck me with whatever he had. His fingers. Dildos. A fucking broom handle. Jimmy's voice. *You or Riley.*

"Stop!" I scream.

"*Shh.*" The shush is a long, slow release of air from a valve. At this point, I breathe again, but barely. I'm scraping at his grip so hard, I have to be drawing blood.

I suck in a breath, my eyes squeezed shut. "Let me go," I manage to get out before his hold tightens again.

"You came here of your own free will, *Bella*. That choice was yours. And for the next week, that choice was your last."

Alarmed, I freeze. "Enzo, please—"

Lightly, he nudges the vibrator along the swell of my ass. "I'm just resting it here. Reminding you why you need to be good." Enzo's gaze lands between my legs. "Pull your panties away. I want to see how wet you are."

I'm not sure which is more mortifying: me getting off on his choke hold, or him seeing me soaking wet. And, soaking wet in the ugliest, plainest white panties known to man.

Once again, his grip tightens until I see stars. The look in his eyes is so hungry. So dark. "Show me," he pleads to my lips.

His voice is so coaxing. So soft. I slide a hand down my body, slowly obeying his command until I hook them and pull them aside, letting him see it. See all of me so bare and vulnerable and wet, I can hardly breathe.

His grip eases up. "Beautiful."

My breaths are fevered as his fingers skate along mine. "Make yourself feel good, *Bella*."

I don't know what comes over me, but part of me wants this. Maybe it's his tone. The way his nostrils flare, desperate to catch a whiff of me from here. Like he's grappling for control and might totally lose it all, if only I touch myself.

In this moment, there's no one else and nothing he wants more. He's coming totally unglued, and all he's doing is watching me.

And in some dark corner of my twisted world, I like being watched.

I start slowly, teasing my skin, the swollen bud of my clit. Tracing pleasure up and down as his jaw clenches tight. "*Mmm*," he growls low.

My back arches without permission. And the words that

come out of my mouth are half delirious, half fuck you. "Is this what you want to see, Mr. D'Angelo?"

"That pretty pussy drips honey and needs to be fucked, *Bella*." I sink into his voice, my body reeling with desire until he says, "Rub yourself. Now."

That's it, fuck that cunt, you filthy whore.

My momentary hesitation earns me the vibrator being turned on. "Wait," I gasp, rushing to do as he says. *Your hand, whore. Or something else goes inside.*

My fingers make pained movements up and down as I bite back tears, desperate to block out his voice—Jimmy's voice. *You're a slut. Just like your mother.*

Enzo nips my neck. Hard. Snapping me back to the present. Air rushes into my lungs, and instantly, I stop.

His gaze pierces mine, igniting shame and fear across my face like wildfire. His fingertips gently graze mine, exerting a soft, subtle pressure.

"This is mine," he lulls, working a coaxing, sensual cadence that smooths away the rough edges and kills all the pain. "You will worship it. As I will worship it. Now, show me what that sweet pussy needs, *Bella*." His kiss is like a drug, intoxicating and addictive. "What you need," he whispers.

Without my permission, my fingers work in tandem with his. A slow exploration that's lava against my skin—shame overshadowed by desire.

Lust.

Need.

Want.

My fingers glide up and down, in and out—rubbing,

rubbing—erasing the thorns and hurt and pain I've felt for so long. Too long.

Cool air hits my breasts, heavy as I feel my blouse being opened, my bra unclasped, and his scruff teasing my naked flesh. His tongue lingers along my skin, and his fingers play in and out of mine.

"Is this what you like, *Bella*?"

Words escape me. I nibble on my lip, surrendering to the feeling of our touch—his touch.

"You're so ready, *Bella*." I hear him through my detached state—caught between a dream and rising nirvana. "Come for me." His fingers work me—then mine—thrusting in and out.

So intense. So goddamn good.

When my nipple is sucked hard, the sensation is blinding. My back whips up, arching as the orgasm rips me apart from the inside out.

A cry of ecstasy pierces the air as I shatter like a glass figurine hit by a baseball bat—a million tiny pieces forever changed, breathless.

I'm only half aware of him removing whatever remains of my clothes. Of his mouth sucking each of my fingers, licking them clean, and savoring the taste.

He kisses his way between my legs. His tongue takes one long lick—a match strike against my core that has me gasping for air.

With a guttural growl, his voice reverberates through the air, igniting a rush of goosebumps and conflicting sensations within me. Authoritative and charged, he's primal. Commanding.

"Again."

Oh, fuck.

CHAPTER 20
Enzo

Damn this woman.

Kennedy could practically make me come in my pants just by looking at her.

I stare down at her, memorizing every line of her face as she breaks. Her walls crash down so spectacularly that the only things left in their wake are lust and sin.

My eyes trace a path along her heavy tits and pert, pink nipples before soaking in every soft, sculpted curve.

She's not skinny, thank fuck. But hours of grueling dance moves keep her body toned yet sensual, and her stamina off the charts.

Part of me says to let her rest. Give her a minute to catch her breath. But that trace of arousal in her eyes is enough for me to say *fuck that*.

"Turn around," I demand. "Show me that gorgeous ass."

Fear flashes across her beautiful face. "What?"

If she's read anything about me, she has every reason to be

scared. Every twisted, sadistic rumor is true. "I'm not fucking your pretty ass, *Bella*." My voice darkens. "Not yet."

"Yet?"

I skate a finger between the glorious mounds of her breasts and past her naval. "In one week, there's no part of this body I won't claim."

I know she hates what I'm doing to her. Hates how good it makes her feel. Her tears tell me that. She bites her lip so hard, I have to lick the blood off her delicious mouth.

Not that it's a fetish or anything. And not because I give a damn about the two thousand dollar sheets we're fucking on. But because triggers are funny things. Seeing her own blood afterwards could breathe life to some demon in her mind.

And we can't have that. Not when her pussy is weeping so sweetly.

I slide a finger into her slick, tight pussy. Then two. When that little whimper of hers turns into a purr, I stop.

"Please," she moans, the feral noise wrapping around my cock like a goddamned fist.

I paint her wetness over her lips before licking it off. "Hands and knees."

A small flood of tears breaks through as she swallows hard. "But—"

"Now, *Bella*," I growl.

Her hesitation is fleeting. Then, she does as she's told, slowly shifting onto her hands and knees.

She blinks away more tears as I count the scars along her back. Thirteen. A fraction of mine, but still thirteen too many. It brings the count to twenty-two, though I'm sure I'll find more.

I trace the ridge of each cigarette burn with my finger, one by one. "Is this what you didn't want me to see?"

Her head falls, in shame, perhaps.

When she doesn't answer, I'm not sure which pisses me off more; her shattered spirt or her silence.

I grip a handful of her hair, tight enough to make her gasp. "Answer me."

"Yes," she says pained. "He did it so no man would want me."

I could press her. Demand to know who he is. But no demon will come between me and *Bella*, and I'm sure as fuck not inviting them our bed.

I force her to face the mirror. "Watch," I growl. "Watch how beautiful your pain looks to me."

Slowly, I pump a finger in and out of her.

Then two.

Then three.

Her body takes control, moving of its own accord, riding my fingers like her cunt's about to swallow my hand as she stares at her reflection in awe.

"That's it," I breathe, feeling her tension build as she soaks me to the bone.

I love how she fucks herself. How her pussy tightens. How she's so close to finally letting go.

"Does my good little girl want to come all over my hand?"

When she doesn't answer, I move my thumb to the crevice of her ass. The shock of sensations slows her rhythm, but doesn't stop.

She can't stop.

"Answer me." The warning in my voice is dark and controlled.

Whatever logic was left dangling in her mind snaps away. "Yes," she pants, obeying me.

"Yes, what?" I fist her hair tighter. "Use your words."

It's strange how much I needed to hear her give consent with her outside voice. To tell me exactly what she wants and how she wants it.

And to know that no one other than me can give it to her.

"Yes," she cries out through raw lust. "I want to come." Her body takes all three fingers deeper. "I want to come. All. Over. Your. Hand."

Fuck me.

Hearing those filthy words come out of her sweet lips nearly has me coming all over my pants.

Her eyes squeeze shut. God, she's so close.

I grip her chin with enough force, her eyes snap wide. "Then open your eyes and fuck me, *Bella*. See what I see. How lovely you are. And how beautiful my sweet little girl is when she comes."

Her moans rise to cries, and then screams. "Enzo!" Her body shudders in waves, her fists clutching the sheets as she crushes my fingers to oblivion.

I should ease up, but I don't.

The tip of my thumb presses into the vulnerable bud of her tight hole, as my deep, punishing thrusts rip an orgasm through her so hard, her body collapses on the bed.

An angel like Kennedy should glide down from heaven and drift through a gentle tide of emotions. But not my *Bella*.

Curled into a ball, the dam finally bursts, unleashing a

torrent of raw, ugly, crashing waves of emotions that an hour of sobbing won't completely wash away.

I want to show her that this is why there is nothing more terrifying than me, and why she should run.

How a week with me will break her.

Will break us both.

Instead, I lick every last drop of her off my fingers and whisper, "Good girl, *Bella*."

Such a goddamned good girl.

CHAPTER 21
Enzo

Fucked.

That's not just what I've done, it's also exactly what I am.

For the past three hours, I've watched my little *Bella* unravel, again and again. *And* again.

On her hand.

On mine.

On my tongue.

And so many times on that little toy that I'm about to have it dipped in gold.

Mmm. A moan erupts from my chest thinking of how good she felt. It took a while for her sweet pussy to take three fingers.

God, how tight will she feel riding my cock?

I lick her sinful taste on my lips—utterly addictive. A deep, satisfied moan rumbles low in my chest.

And yet, I'm far from satisfied.

That initial twist of her lips wasn't pleasure, which pisses me off. Whatever ghost from Kennedy's past that dared intrude in my bed just gave me another enemy to hunt.

Whoever he is, he's a dead man walking. And his death will be slow. Ridding him of his skin one agonizing strip at a time will take so long he'll probably die half-way through it.

I sip my scotch, letting the heat linger as it chases the last of *Bella's* essence down my throat. Exterminating whatever vermin inflicted this pain will happen one way or another. But scrubbing every lingering trace of him from *Bella's* mind?

That takes more than a thirst for blood and a wet team.

It will take time, and time is the only luxury I don't have.

Frustrated, I exhale sharply, shifting uncomfortably in my seat.

Despite moving to the main cabin and keeping my ass away from her, the temptation of sinking into her tight sex is too much. My thoughts keep circling back to her like a flock of vultures, starving for more.

Because of all the ways I've defiled *Bella's* breathtaking body, not once did I do it with my dick.

I flip through my phone, burying myself in absolutely everything except *Bella's* slick, tight cunt, and my cock is not happy. Not happy at all.

The damned thing is seconds from tearing out of my slacks like the Hulk.

My jaw clenches. I had her, damn it.

I could've fucked her to my heart's content. Driven myself so deep into heaven, my dick would've left with a halo. Fucked Kennedy Luciano right out of my system for good, with a week to spare.

But... I didn't.

Why?

Because she's not ready.

I pinch the bridge of my nose, perplexed. Why am I fixated on *Bella* being ready? Women are always ready.

Always!

And it wasn't as if I was about to dry-fuck her. That serene geyser between her legs proves she's more than ready.

Ugh. I wipe a hand down my face. When was the last time I had a woman melting like hot cream in my hands and not had her on all fours, kowtowing to my needy dick?

And my dick definitely has needs. Ask around.

Disgusted, I shake my head. *Who am I?*

"I'm the one who cured *Bella's* fear of flying, that's who I am," I mutter angrily to myself.

"Did you say something, Mr. D'Angelo?" The groggy-eyed dog trainer yawns from her seat, though I'm not sure where the dog is. Speaking of which, where's he supposed to shit?

Scanning the space, I spot a small patch of grass apparently growing out of the floor. I'm not sure how, but okay.

Her gaze holds mine as I nod, her smile growing weirder by the second.

My phone lights up with an incoming call.

Sin

"*Shit*," I huff. If he's calling at this hour, it can't be good.

Which means as much as I don't want to talk to him, I need to take his call. *Besides, if ever there was a way to kill a boner...*

I adjust myself and shift in my seat before answering. "Let me guess. Another paternity claim?" Which would be an outrageous lie. My dick hasn't wanted anything but Kennedy in months.

Or, for the year before her.

The mere thought of sinking into her warm, soft body, naked and snuggled beneath a blanket, has him twitching again. And yet, I resist the urge to hang up the phone. I refrain from rushing back there, from bending her into any position I desire...

To take, take, take...

"Paternity test?" Sin scoffs, his voice dripping with skepticism. "Why? Has the woman you've kidnapped already filed a claim?"

I roll my eyes and do what I do best: deflect. "You're slipping, Sin. I did not kidnap Savannah Whitaker. Check my books. Her services are paid for. At three times the going rate."

"I mean the other woman you kidnapped," he says, his words slicing through my bullshit like a samurai sword through butter. I'm poised with a dozen more lies when he adds, "The one with the dog."

I swear, Dante's mouth has a date with duct tape if he doesn't stop narcing to Sin. Clearing my throat, I respond with forced composure. "I have not kidnapped her. She's my guest."

"Well, if she is who I think she is, the pleasure of her company has an expiration date."

I sit up. "Who do you think she is?"

"Kennedy Luciano." Tension grips my neck with the way he says her name—as if he knows her—until he adds, "Jimmy Luciano's daughter."

"Step-daughter," I seethe. Is he the one who left those scars?

Because I will happily leave him sitting in a vat of acid up to his neck, just to relish in his screams.

"Andre called. Reminding you that this little escapade lasts one week, or—"

"Or what, Sin?" I interrupt, my voice a tight, low coil, ready to strike. "He should know better than to threaten me. I don't need an excuse to go to war with my uncle."

"No, but he needs one to go to war with you. And if this girl is riling you up the way I think she is, she's it." After a tense moment, his tone softens, paternal and pleading. "She owes him."

"Her dirtbag stepfather owed him. Not her." My argument tastes weak and bitter.

"And considering Jimmy Luciano is missing or dead, the debt falls to her. Period. Unless you have a claim," Sin counters, his words tinged with hope. "Do you?"

My response is clipped. "No," I huff. The fact that Kennedy Luciano and her worthless stepfather are the only ones in Chicago who aren't indebted to me boggles my fucking mind.

"Will Andre sell her to you?"

"Absolutely. For D'Angelo Holdings or my head on a platter. Or both."

"Then send her back," he insists. "Before you get attached." This is the point of the conversation I always hate with Sin. When his voice softens, sickly with so much paternal marshmallowyness, I nearly gag on it.

My silence is enough for him to switch from a carrot to a stick.

"You, more than anyone, know this game. We collect on our debts, and we don't interfere with how others collect on theirs."

More silence.

"You, yourself, enforce these very rules every goddamned day."

His words sting like a slap. He's not wrong. While some kings rule from their thrones, I'm down in the trenches, sleeves rolled up, hands dirty.

It's exactly how I prefer it. Violence soothes me in ways very little else does. If you want a calm, rational mind, you go to Smoke. But if you want results, and don't care how you get them, you come to me.

And sooner or later, everyone always comes to me.

Though, unlike my douchebag uncle, I've never held a debt against a woman or child.

Besides, going after women and children achieves nothing. From what I've seen, most of them have been tortured enough. And since I'm neither an asshole nor a coward, I have better outlets for my rage.

Lashing out on poor, defenseless victims is my uncle's domain. He and his mangy dog, Rocco.

A deep wound rips wide in the center of my chest. The mere thought of Rocco laying a finger on *Bella* sends a shockwave through me so intense that the sound of the phone's screen cracking in my hand brings me back to Sin's voice droning on.

"Nothing good can come of this. Just walk away, Enzo. You've been sleep-deprived for months, and you're not thinking clearly. You need a break."

"You're right," I give in. "And I'm taking a break. In Italy. For seven uninterrupted days."

"Will you at least be back for the wedding?" he asks, his tone kicking up hope against a solid wall of *don't give a fuck*.

And while I'd usually have hung up by now, I know what he's doing. Gauging just how far off the deep end I've flown. "Why don't you ask me what you really want to know?"

"And what do I really want to know?" he asks, his voice lifting with all that maniacal psychoanalysis crap he loves pulling on me.

"You're wondering if at the end of a week, I'll give her back." I shrug to myself. "Maybe. Or perhaps I'll keep her. She seems cozy, holed up in my spider's web. Meanwhile, we'll cut through all the polite bullshit while I joyfully declare war."

CHAPTER 22
Enzo

I CAN JUST IMAGINE Sin's face scoffing through the phone. "You? Threatening war over a woman? Don't forget, Enzo. The problem with war is that it's exhilarating at first—"

"*Mmm.* Yes, when the bloodbath tastes like fresh victory on the tongue," I say, bathing in the thought of it.

"But then, around the time you realize the blood on your hands is ours, that gluttonous rush will end. It could be anyone, Enzo—Smoke, Dante, any one of your brothers—"

"Don't forget me, Sin," I snipe back. "Maybe you'll finally be rid of me for good."

"Or, God forbid, Trinity," he adds, stabbing me in the gut, then twisting the knife. "Think it through. Take a week and whatever else you need from this girl. Then give her to Andre and get on with your life."

I swallow hard. Deep down, I know my time with Kennedy is borrowed. One week. That's it. Then I hand her back to Andre to do with as he pleases.

But what if I won't? I can't?

I gag my conscience and kick him under the rug. "Speaking of which," I say, "I don't have a will. Be a sport, Sin. Draft me up one. You know, just in case."

"Good news. I already have, Enzo. You've left everything to Uncle Andre. Just in case."

"What?"

"You and I were in a fight," he explains, and I realize he's not fucking around. "You'd just accessed my phone, changed a bunch of ringtones to breathy climax screams—one male," he points out.

I smile. I also scanned all his emails, activated his tracker, and loaded a ton of spyware—which is how I know about my own father's will—but he doesn't need to know all that.

"Besides," he continues. "Andre gifted you a girl. For a week. I figured it had to be what you wanted, considering you always were his favorite."

"Do not piss me off," I warn.

"Give me your word you'll be at Smoke's wedding, and I'll draft up a new one, ready for your signature."

With a resigned sigh, I suppress the simmering rage beneath the surface long enough to avoid going another nine rounds with Sin. "I'll be there."

"Good. Enjoy your week. If you start getting attached—"

I hang up before he can pester me for the millionth time about sending Kennedy back, like she's some Amazon impulse buy I regret.

Kennedy's no trinket. She's a diamond. One I have claimed.

I run a hand over my face, unsettled. My uncle is many things—calculated and lazy tie for first—but benevolent? He'd no sooner gift me a woman for a week than spread his cheeks and have Rocco fuck him in the ass.

In our world, there are no gifts, only trades. We exchange threats veiled as pleasantries, manipulate people like pawns, and always, without fail, demand one thing in return: blood.

Eventually, Uncle Andre will come for my blood, looking to drain me like a goddamned vampire. But for now, he's just buttering me up.

He thinks seven days with Kennedy will be a slow drip of opioids—mainlined, raw, and addictive. And so sweet, I'll never be able to slice her from my veins.

I sip my scotch. Is he right?

I drop my head back to the seat and shut my eyes. The pain has started, radiating like shards of glass behind my eyes and down my neck. I swear, licking barbed wire would be less painful.

When I hear a skittered sound from behind me, my tired body reacts on instinct. I reach for my gun when two hands trail down my shoulders and arms. Instead of easing the tension, they manage to make it so much worse.

I think it's her perfume. Savannah wears some god-awful stench she probably paid a thousand dollars a bottle for. Her frigid fingers begin working deep massages into my shoulders as I try not to gag.

"What's the matter?" Savannah purrs. Her eyes linger on my slacks as she moistens her lips suggestively. "Feeling a bit . . . pent-up?"

As a matter of fact, yes. So much so that beneath my slacks, I'm in physical pain. Agony and desperate for a release.

But the thought of pressing into anyone but *Bella* stings

like acid on bare skin. Clenching my jaw, I force out through gritted teeth, "I'm fine."

"I'm very discrete," she hushes, her invitation breathy against my neck. "Your little girlfriend will never know." Savannah drops to her knees, her ample tits on full display. "You're so tense," she pouts, her hands sliding up my thighs to my belt and begins to unfasten it.

I lean in. "And you're so close," I whisper with a grin, "to having your hands ripped off and turned into chew toys if they don't quit pawing at my fine Italian leather."

A nervous giggle escapes her lips, her fingers retreating completely. She stands. "Well, if you need me for anything—"

"Oh, make no mistake, Ms. Whitaker, I do need you," I say even-toned. "I need you to take care of the dog. If that's not your purpose here, then consider yourself excess baggage. Which I can easily dispose of to lighten the load."

She scuttles back to her chair, a gust of anxiety and nerves as I watch her retreat.

Finally, some peace.

The sharp pain travels from the base of my spine to my temples like daggers scraping against bone. Even the two scotches I've had aren't dulling it, and the conversation with Sin has only managed to make it ten times worse.

With a sigh, I toss my phone aside, sinking back into my chair and closing my eyes, desperate for relief.

Or, to black out.

A warm breath skates along my knee, eliciting a whole-body wince. I swear, this woman is inching closer to getting tossed out somewhere over the Atlantic.

Before I can utter another threat, a disgustingly wet sneeze shoots across my lap. My eyes snap wide open.

The dog's brow quirks, accompanied by an ear twitch—just the one.

I blink. Gross.

I nudge him away with my foot. "Do not make me kill you," I warn.

A pathetically small growl escapes him, followed by a bark that pierces my ear like a prison shank.

I pinch the bridge of my nose. I don't need this.

When he hops up and licks my hands, an unexpected warmth spreads through me like hot caramel over an apple.

Like so many things that dare to stir even a flicker of light in the deep crevices of my chest, instantly, I loathe it.

I whip around, eager to locate Savannah and make her handle this situation. I swear, that woman has one job. One.

"Where the fuck is she?"

CHAPTER 23
Kennedy

Thump.

I snap awake, every muscle protesting as I struggle to orient myself.

In the dimness, it takes precious seconds to shake off the sleep-induced haze.

Where the hell am I?

The soft hum of the engine reminds me I'm not in Kansas anymore. Or even Chicago.

Instead, I find myself nestled in luxurious silk sheets, surrounded by the scent of sweat, sex, and Enzo's intoxicating cologne.

Slowly, realization sinks in. I'm still on a plane, suspended somewhere over a dark, boundless stretch of ocean, and strangely, I'm not afraid.

With a deep inhale, the fear that overshadowed me earlier—or for most of my life—is gone.

I roll to my back and feel it. Pain—a pervasive ache that

courses across every inch of my body. I feel like my mind, body, and soul have been hit by a Mack truck . . . especially between my legs.

I draw in a sharp breath, easing out of the emotional overload of the last few hours.

Floral notes fill my lungs with each deep inhale. I shift and come face-to-face with it: a plump red rose.

It's resting on the pillow beside me. Apparently, Enzo's a man of many talents, including pulling flowers out his butt.

Lazily, my finger dusts the petals, and I take another lingering whiff before throwing an arm over my face.

It feels like I'm plummeting from the top of a skyscraper, free-falling with a clear view of the concrete street below, wondering how to drag out every second.

Argh. I'm falling for him.

For a long stretch, I lie there. In his bed. Alone.

Enzo D'Angelo has wrecked me. Emotionally and physically, inside and out. Every muscle in my body aches from the aftermath of God's gift to multiple orgasms.

Seriously, I know why there's a website dedicated to Enzo *fucking* D'Angelo. He makes *fucking* both a science and an art, and my body is still reeling from that last one. It was so blindingly intense, I know that walking will pose a serious challenge.

And yet, not once did he please himself.

No hand job.

No dry humping.

Nothing.

What man does that?

One who should be sainted.

Absentmindedly, my fingers trace the rumpled sheets beside me. The man stripped me of my clothes and common sense. At one point, he had me climb onto his face and move like I was neck-and-neck for first place in a bull-riding contest. Yet the most he shed was his tie.

His tie!

Enzo has control freak written all over him in big, bold graffiti, and all I want to do is scrape it off.

With my tongue.

Shut up.

It's fucked up that he grabbed me by the throat. But what's even more fucked up is that my body responded. I didn't want him to stop, and that pisses me off.

If I'm aroused by a twisted, arrogant, sadist, what does that make me?

I shake my head. Clearly, I have issues.

"One week." A whisper cuts through the darkness, sharp and hushed.

Huh?

I glance at the bathroom door, edged in a faint glow of light.

It's a private bathroom with marble counters, gold fixtures, and Netflix. An over-the-top indulgent space fit for a king. I know because I've become well acquainted with it between sex-a-thon sprints, and frankly, I could've lived in there.

This time, the whisper is louder and more urgent. It's a woman's voice. "That's what he said."

I step off the bed, my gaze snagging on a smoking jacket draped over the corner. I don't remember that being there before. Did Enzo leave this for me?

Slipping it on, it smells like fresh laundry and swaddles me like an angel cloud. Not gonna lie—I could get used to this.

I move to the door and press an ear to it, straining to catch the conversation. A few snippets bleed through. "Yes. That's what I heard." Who's she talking to? My hand lands on the handle when I hear, "He's got her for a week. Then he's ditching her."

My heart clogs my throat. Me. She's talking about me. Which is fine, I guess. It wasn't like Enzo dropped to one knee, professing his undying eternal love.

So why does it feel like someone's wringing every last drop of emotion from my chest?

Maybe because the sting of his stubble is still fresh between my legs.

I steel my heart. He paid off a debt—a big one. Shouldn't that be enough? This is probably just a normal business transaction from one dangerous mobster to countless women seeking his help.

If enduring a week of being ravaged by Enzo is what it takes to see Riley, then so be it.

Especially if he ravages me like that.

Shut up.

And sure, I agreed of my own free will. But he conveniently omitted the part about broadcasting it to the whole damn world —especially to Savannah.

Who seems to have taken it upon herself to be the town crier. Her tone softens slightly, and I lean in, trying to catch every whispered syllable.

When she says, "All I know is that he's not putting this woman over his family. And why would he? She's nobody."

Nobody? Tough talk from a high-heeled pooper scooper.

She then adds, "Of course, he hit on me."

He did?

And it's all I can do to resist the urge to storm in, snatch her phone, and shove it up her pompous ass, all while saying, *"Back off, bitch. He's mine."*

Instead, I draw in a deep breath and remind myself that *he* isn't mine. In fact, men like Enzo can never be owned. It's the reason they're so damned good in bed.

Even so, I yank the door open, wresting the phone from her perfectly manicured claws. "You can't do that!" she snaps, visibly affronted.

Glancing at the phone, I see "Caller unknown" flashing on the screen, but there's a number. A number I recognize, but from where? Is it Andre? The press? "Who is this?" I demand, my voice sharp with suspicion.

Before I can get an answer, a long, exasperated sigh fills the line, followed by the abrupt click of the call ending. Savannah's self-satisfied smirk only adds fuel to the fire burning inside me. "Who were you talking to?" I shout.

Savannah's hand clamps over my mouth. "Keep your voice down," she hisses, locking the door behind me.

"How did you get in here?"

"*Shh*," she hushes me, plucking a bobby pin from her hair. "It's not exactly a vault. I just needed some breathing space, and you were out cold. Speaking of which, if you don't keep your voice down and Mr. D'Angelo hears you, you're dead."

Do I look like an idiot? It suddenly dawns on me where I've seen that number before.

On a business card. The one pressed into my hand by

Special Agent Caleb Knox. Riley's old roommate's cousin. Every few weeks, he leaves a message for me to call. And every few weeks, I've ignored him.

I square my jaw. "I believe you mean if Enzo hears me, *you're* the one in hot water. See, I'm not the one ratting him out to the Feds."

The color drains from her high-set cheeks, her once-pleasant smile fading into oblivion. "Please. If you tell him, I'm as good as dead."

"Then explain why Agent Knox is keeping tabs on him," I demand.

She stares at me, confusion etched across her features. "They're not. They're watching you."

"Me?" She's lying, she has to be. "Why would anyone be watching me? I'm nobody." She said so herself.

Her shrug is dismissive. "I don't know. All I do know is that Enzo has you for a week." Leaning in, she adds, "Seems like you're on loan."

"I'm not a library book," I retort back. I'm not sure how much she had to drink, but none of what she says makes sense. "Yes, there was a debt, but Enzo paid it."

She retrieves a tube of lipstick from her clutch with casual indifference. "Are you absolutely certain?" she asks, her eyes fixed on her reflection in the mirror as she carefully applies the dark cherry red. "Why would he?"

As much as this woman is practically begging for an ass-kicking, her question needles my chest.

Savannah pulls a pouty face in the mirror before continuing. "I overheard Mr. D'Angelo on the phone. His uncle's demands are just too steep. He gets one week with you, then . . ." her words trail off as she fixes a smudge.

"And then?" I push, my heart racing with dread and disbelief.

Her next words land like a punch to the gut, knocking all the air from my lungs. "Then, he gives you back. Like a wad of used gum, I guess." My back hits the wall for support as panic claws its way up my spine. My mind races, replaying those words over and over again.

Then he gives me back.

A strange calm settles over me as emotions clash for control, like I'm standing in the eye of a storm. My father warned me that caving to panic or fear only drag you down faster. So I cling to the only thing that fuels me forward.

With both hands, I latch onto hate.

I despise Enzo D'Angelo for what he's about to do—sweep me off my feet just to toss me into the depths of hell.

And what about Riley? Can I trust him to keep his word? To keep her safe?

With my father's determination at my back, my eyes lock with Savannah's. "Tell me everything you know."

She sweeps her long bangs from her face. "What makes you think I know anything?"

The white mini-Birkin on the counter catches my eye. I grab it and dangle it over the toilet. "Talk, or your pet alligator gets a nice, blue bath."

"Okay, okay." Both hands shoot up in surrender. "I don't know much, just that there's something about your name."

My name? "Kennedy?"

"No." She lets out a frustrated breath. "Your other name. Your *real* name."

My brows knit together hard. Confused, I repeat her words. "My real name?"

"Mellow? Ménage?"

My heart drops as my father's proud Scottish name rises from the center of my chest to my lips. "Mullvain."

CHAPTER 24
Enzo

WHEN I GLANCE AROUND, Savannah Whitaker has magically vanished. Shocker. She's probably hiding out in the bathroom, doing her best to avoid being tossed from the plane.

Which, with this dog using my fine wool suit as his personal sneeze guard, she should be scared shitless.

I shut my eyes tight, desperate to ignore both the scrap of fur at my feet and the jabbing pain at my skull.

His little paw batting at my knee makes that all but impossible. For a fleeting second, I picture drop-kicking the ball of fur into the cockpit.

Which would be followed by the glow of Kennedy's murderous glare, so I refrain. He does it again. "Fuck off," I mutter.

When I hear the delicate rip of his unclipped nail against my expensive slacks, I snap, "What?"

Without asking, the dog backs up, gives his rear end a shake, and jumps into my lap. Like his nickname is *Death Wish*.

My eyes narrow. "You've got three seconds. Choose to live, mutt."

He doesn't budge. With an exasperated sigh, I shove the dog off my lap and smooth out my slacks. He barks, and it takes a beat to realize I'm locked in a serious death glare with a dog.

My phone buzzes with a text, snapping me from my staring contest with Fido. The incoming text displays an anonymous sender and only a single number for the message.

7

Ah, my uncle, right on time. Apparently, he plans to remind me of my remaining time with *Bella*—on a daily basis, no doubt.

Or, maybe the cocksucker just wants to brag that he can actually count to seven, because I seriously had my doubts.

I down a gulp of scotch, annoyed.

Maybe it's Rocco, peddling his usual brand of mind fucks, relishing in the cheap thrill of messing with my head.

Regardless of who sent the message, it elicits the same response: blinding, unadulterated rage.

With a muttered curse, I hurl my phone against the nearest wall, down the rest of my drink, and shut my eyes tight.

Seven days.

With most women, seven days is six days too many. But this is Kennedy, and I already know it won't be nearly enough.

I like to think I can afford anything. Assets. Loyalties. Souls. But a war?

Putting Trinity's safety on the line again?

Even I have my limits. And keeping my sister tucked away

and safe is it. She's been to the pit of hell and back again. Trinity's been through enough.

But then again, so have I.

Where there's a will, there's a way the lunatic Scotsman whispers in my ear.

And, as usual, he's right.

Where there's a will, a psychopath, and the net worth of a mid-size European country, there's a way.

There's always a way.

Always.

Visions of her in a white dress give way to a night of her on her knees, and I groan in actual need. Raw, unrelenting, visceral pain.

Half the time, I struggle just to breathe under the weight of my own skin, and the woman is pure oxygen.

And the thought of losing her? Fuck, hacking off both legs at the knees and hobbling around on stumps would be less excruciating.

I sprint through several options and blow out a reflective breath. The weight of four paws hops up on my lap. His persistence would almost be admirable, in the way one admires Kamikaze bombers.

Where's the *Wicked Witch of the West?* I've got a dog she might be interested in.

I pinch the bridge of my nose, eyes still closed. "Look, Toto, I don't care how attached Kennedy is to you. Get off my lap before I have you made into smoking slippers."

Nothing.

He doesn't budge.

Then he paws at my shirt. My *silk* shirt. I'm two seconds from stuffing him into the overhead bin when I open my eyes.

What the...

In his mouth is my phone. Gingerly, he sets it on my lap. A message lights up the cracked light of the screen, and I'm glad it's not from Uncle Fuckface or his sidekick.

It's from the only person who somehow always melts my pain to tolerable.

> **TRINITY**
> I thought I was your favorite sister.

The corners of my lips lift to a smile.

> **ME**
> You're my only sister.
>
> Favorite is implied.

> **TRINITY**
> Since when do you have a dog?
>
> And why am I the last to know?
>
> And you named her Truffles???

She follows it with a string of heart emojis, which pretty much solidifies it. "Good news, dog. You get to live."

He blinks, utterly clueless.

I narrow my gaze at said dog as the phone rings. A video request. "What kind of name is Truffles?" I ask, disgusted, flipping his ear. "You're a dude. Have some respect," I say as if he had any choice in the matter.

I let the phone ring twice more before I answer, fluffing

Truffle's fur just so. As soon as I do, Trinity's squeal is so loud I'm now permanently deaf in one ear.

Truffles tilts his head, and my sister coos at the stupidly adorable pup.

I nuzzle him closer to my face, hoping to elicit a broader smile from Trinity. "She's so precious." Truffles responds with a sloppy lick to my cheek.

Bleh.

Try as I might, I can't mask the disgust seeping from every one of my pores, prompting a giggle from Trinity louder than any I've heard in years.

It squeezes my heart just enough that I have to blurt out, "He."

"Huh?" she asks, confused.

"It's a *he*," I explain, lifting him up so she can thoroughly inspect his junk.

She winces and averts her eyes until I set him back down. "You"—she points to the screen—"named a boy dog *Truffles*?"

"You named a girl cat *Thor*."

"I was three. And in my defense, Thor was a huge cat."

She's spot-on with that. He's like a colossal Maine Coon, but with extra fluff. A memory pops into my head. "Remember when you tried to ride him?"

Her laughter fades quickly. "I don't remember that," she confesses, her teeth worrying her lip, a habit she falls into when she trips over a chasm in her memory.

It's become a regular part of her life, something she's learned to accept. But for me, it slices a deep gash in my heart the way it does every fucking time. The fact that she remembers any of us or even her own name feels like a miracle.

Her attacker managed to wipe memories from her mind like an eraser. I intend on returning the favor. With a power drill.

I veil my anger under a warm grin. "You were very young."

"No, I'm just losing my mind." Her laughter is a brittle echo of what it used to be, and it cuts through me like broken glass.

Grasping at straws, I clutch at the only one I have—the damn dog.

I hold his paw to the screen and pull a British accent out of my ass.

"You're mad," I declare aloud.

She blinks. "W-what?"

"Bonkers, completely off your head!" I push Truffles closer to the screen. "But I'll tell you a secret."

"*All the best people are*," she says. A warm rush of color returns to her cheeks as she finishes the Lewis Carrol quote, adding, "*Alice's Adventures in Wonderland*." She nods with relief. A small victory against the demons of her past.

I puppet around the little dog ridiculously, ventriloquist-like, as if I've shoved my hand up his butt. "Who painted my roses red? Off with their heads!"

In that shared laughter, time stands still, cocooning us in a bubble where time blurs and pain recedes.

She's not a victim, and I'm not the blood-thirsty monster hell-bent on vengeance.

Here, now, I'm just her older brother, doing stupid things so my little sister isn't sad. Her laughter fades to four simple words: "I love you, Zo."

What's left of my heart wrings out four words in response. "I love you, too."

CHAPTER 25
Kennedy

I LOVE YOU, too.

My steps grind to a halt as I digest Enzo's words. Adding insult to injury, he's not just returning me. He's also head over heels in love with another woman—a drop-dead gorgeous stunner, by the way—which only rubs salt in a big, gaping wound.

And apparently, Enzo's way of wooing his beloved involves parading my dog around like a muppet. It would actually be ridiculously adorable if it didn't make me want to projectile vomit all over his plush private jet.

The man just spent the better part of three hours pleasuring me to the point of carpel tunnel, and now he loves *her*? What am I? His fluffer?

Ugh. Never mind that he's about to return me to Andre, and by extension, Rocco.

Though that could explain why he didn't actually seal the deal? Because fucking me with his dick is off-limits?

I'd rather die than let Rocco touch me again.

I take a deep, thoughtful breath. Admittedly, going head-to-head with a dangerous thug isn't exactly smart. Especially considering I can't exactly catch the next bus home.

Not that I give a damn about what happens to me. My sole focus is Riley. *Stay calm.*

I struggle to keep my fists at bay, the expensive fabric of his smoking jacket bearing the brunt of my clenched hands. Because when my mind buckles beneath the crushing weight of emotional overload, restraint isn't an option.

Like my father used to say, "*Hell hath no fury like a Scottish lass scorned.*"

But before I unleash raw rage all over his D'Angelo ass, the beautiful blonde on FaceTime catches sight of me. "Who's that?" she asks, her blue eyes wide.

Enzo whirls around, with the woman on the phone in one hand and Truffles in the other.

I bat my eyes and wonder just how he'll explain me away—the half-naked mistress to his unsuspecting love. "Yes, Enzo, who am I?"

Instantly, Enzo flashes an unexpected grin, my dog looks oblivious, and the woman on the screen appears to be ecstatic. Sheesh, I guess someone's expecting a hefty settlement in their divorce proceedings.

His gaze pierces mine. "I'll call you back," he says to the woman. With a decisive click, he silences her protests. As he drops Truffles onto the chair and strides into my personal space, his gaze intensifying. "You're up."

"And you're an asshole."

A smirk dances across his lips, revealing a dimple. "Glad you finally got the memo."

I keep my arms tightly crossed against my chest. First, he lies about settling Jimmy's debt, and now he's spinning even more lies to whoever the hell that was—wife, girlfriend, favorite mistress. *Ugh*. I don't know, and I don't care. Instead, I demand, "Take me home."

His smirk morphs into a grin. "No."

This man makes me thermonuclear.

I push into his space, jabbing a finger right into his solid chest, emphasizing every word. "I said *Take. Me. Home.* Now!"

He settles into a seat, thoroughly amused. "And I said no." My treacherous dog hops onto his lap.

I'm about to really lay into him when the flight attendant interrupts with that sickly sweet voice of hers. "Champagne?"

"No," I bark.

"Yes, thank you." Enzo accepts the glass, then pets Truffles. The idiot looks every bit of an evil villain with his pampered pet. "Ms. Luciano needs one," Enzo adds smugly.

"He's right, Ms. Luciano," the flight attendant says. I'm two seconds from giving both of them two big, fat pieces of my mind when she adds, "It's our last service before we land."

Land?

Just then, the plane jerks roughly, sending my heart thumping as I scramble to my seat. The flight attendant clicks the seatbelt in as if I'm a toddler.

"Mullvain," I breathe, tightening my belt until I can't feel my legs.

"Sorry?" she asks.

"My name. It's not Luciano." My death glare turns to Enzo. "It's Mullvain."

"Of course. Ms. Mullvain," she repeats softly with a helpless smile.

I shouldn't take it out on her. It's not her fault she works for a total tool. One who's apparently treating me to the lap of luxury just before dumping me out like yesterday's trash, complete with all the dignity of blue airline waste.

With a small chuckle, Enzo clears his throat. "Mullvain," he utters, shaking his head to himself, and I can't tell if he's angry or amused.

I know he's dangerous, but in this moment, I don't care. When he smirks, I snap. "Something funny?"

Ignoring my question, he continues with deliberate, unhurried movements, placing Truffles gently on the floor.

I watch in awe as my dog seamlessly returns to his seat, curling up on it like he was born to live this life.

Beside him is Savannah, cocooned under a blanket, as if she's been there the whole damn time, blissfully asleep.

I guess we'll just pretend she didn't just reveal that I'm somehow the key to bringing down the D'Angelos.

Enzo then hands me the glass I just refused. "It's either you enjoy some champagne and we talk, or I teach you a lesson."

"A lesson?"

"Yes, *Bella*. A lesson. On what happens when you direct all that blazing hot anger at me."

There's a certain spark in his eyes. A challenge. It's enough of a warning, I know I should back down.

Stupidly, I don't. "Is that before or after another man fucks me?"

He pauses, mid-drink.

His expression turns contemplative, as if weighing a decision. The tension between us is palpable, stretched so thin and tight that I know I'm forcing his hand.

Keep me or cut me loose—it's his family or me.

Then, his eyes land on mine, and his hand flies forward and grabs my hair so swiftly, I gasp.

I can't resist him. Not that I'm trying...

Somehow, the black-and-blue stain across his cheek only intensifies the heat behind his eyes, accentuating his thick brows and full lips. Making him both dangerous and gorgeous at once—even when he's pissed.

"Enzo," I whimper.

"That's right, *Bella*. It's my name you'll speak in vain—and in pleasure. If another man touches you, he loses a limb. If he fucks you, he loses his life. And if you don't know by now, that you are owned—*by me*—by the end of this week, you will."

No more words. No more talk. His lips crash on mine with such force—such possession—there's no way to fight it.

I'm backed into a corner, with nothing but his dominance and my determination to survive him for the next week.

Seven days where Enzo owns me. Controls me. Does whatever the hell he wants to me.

And seven days where I give in.

I'm not doing this for me. I'm doing this for Riley.

I have one week to find a way to break free. For me and my sister to actually escape the reach of the D'Angelo's.

Forever.

Epilogue | Enzo

Mullvain.

It's not her voice that echoes in my mind when that name is spoken.

Like the Scottish ghost of Christmas past, it's his.

His voice always haunts me: a fervent reminder of my conscience and the echoes of my sin.

Father Malone was right. If Kennedy was just some insignificant nobody, my uncle would've named his price. A real price. Not some life or death bullshit game.

Or, knowing him as I truly do, he'd have sold her months ago. Even if only to spite me.

Her being a Mullvain introduces a complication I hadn't anticipated. It means my conniving uncle is banking on this going one of two ways . . .

Either Kennedy dies by my hands, or . . .

I die by hers.

I sink into her mouth and the way she's melting into our kiss. God, even when she's ablaze with unbridled fury, she's stunning. Beautiful and broken. A shattered masterpiece for my soul to put back together.

Kennedy Mullvain will be the death of me.

I don't give a fuck that she deserves a knight in shining armor to sweep her off her feet, slay her demons, and carry her far from my darkness.

Unfortunately for *Bella*, her path crossed mine. The temptation to keep her is too overpowering. My heart lives to latch onto hers, hook after merciless hook, until they beat as one.

I'll perch her on the highest pedestal so she can watch as I obliterate any man that comes near her and annihilate any world without her in it.

I'll carve out my rare, beating heart, serve it up on a platter, and present it at her feet.

In that aspect, for once, my uncle was right.

My death will be her decision.

Just as her father's death was mine.

Thank you for reading ***SINS & Lies***, the second book in the trilogy! Enzo and Kennedy's story continues in ***SINS & Temptation***.

Preorder ***SINS & Temptation*** today!

>> SINS & Temptation

And if you missed other stories in the series, here they are!
SINS of the Syndicate
SINS & Ivy

SINS: The Debt

SINS: The Deal
SINS & Lies
>> **SINS & Temptation**

NEED ANOTHER ANGSTY ROMANCE? TRY OUT THE Boys of Bishop Mountain!
1-CLICK>> MARKED

Eight years ago I nearly died.
And it wasn't that I didn't remember her.
I didn't recognize her. There's a difference.

She was a kid.
And I was a soldier . . .
Two seconds from deploying with her brother for our third, and final, tour.
One I wasn't sure I'd be coming back from.

She thinks I don't remember.
That kiss was beautiful. Innocent.
It kept me alive when I thought it might be my last.
How could I ever forget?

So, shove me off all you want, country girl.
Because you've just landed in my sights,

And you're about to be mine.

1-CLICK>> MARKED
KEEP GOING FOR A SNEAK PEEK >>

Ready for Alex Drake and his obsession, Madison?

1 billionaire.
1 month.
1 bed.

<u>Get The Alex Drake Collection Now></u>

★★★★★ *"What a fabulously sexy hot read!!!" Top 40 Goodreads Reviewer*

★★★★★ *"Talk about heat!! 5 Burning Stars!!!" Amazon Reviewer*

Join Lexxi's VIP reader list to be the first to know of new releases, free books, special prices, and other giveaways!

Free hot romances & happily ever afters delivered to your inbox.
https://www.lexxijames.com/freebies

SINS of the Syndicate

BOOK 1 IN THE SINS SERIES

CHAPTER 1

Ivy

"I'M HERE to see Ms. Palmer."

The man's voice is deep, with an authority that makes me wonder why he requested his tour of the assisted living center with me. His suit is expensive but not overly fitted. And the dark gray is a stark contrast to the clear blue of his eyes. The silvery accents in his well-trimmed salt-and-pepper hair give him the air of distinction, with professional charm brimming from behind what seems to be a practiced smile.

It's not unlike the smiles I'm used to from people clinging to their courtesy as they navigate a world of decisions. How will I care for my loved one? Will they be safe? Is this covered by insurance? How much will it cost?

If money is no object, the ones with the deepest pockets land here. Except for me. It took two years for me to work off my mom's debt, and it gave me a lifetime's worth of watching people in return. I remind myself that I'm here to ease them into a relationship of trust and support. Not to pressure them with a hard sell, despite those very words from my boss.

"I'm Ivy," I say, stepping out from behind the long reception desk. I hold out a hand, meeting his solemn smile with one of my own as he takes my hand for a brief shake. "And you're Mr.—"

"Sin," he says, scanning the lobby and halls. I can't tell if he's overwhelmed or underwhelmed, but he avoids meeting my eyes as he glances around. "Call me Sin."

"All right, *Sin*."

I've already seen the roster, noting that the tour request was made by a Bryce Jacob Sinclair, Esquire. The formal name suits him as equally as the nickname Sin. A gravity and authority harden the lines of his face, hiding whatever's lurking just below the surface.

The heaviness that drags him down threatens to pull me with it, an occupational hazard to a career dependent on emotional connection and empathy. When his expectant eyes meet mine, I snap back to work.

Handing him a visitor badge, I gesture down the north hall. "This way."

Along our tour, Sin asks the usual questions: How many occupants are there? What's the caregiver-to-resident ratio? If the staff live on the premises—which feels more like he's asking if *I* live on the premises.

No matter how many times I give this tour, I'm delighted when he asks about the one thing that always connects us, though it never seems to at first. Mr. Whiskers.

The small fluffy toy is weightless in my hand as I tug it from the pocket it's been peeking out from and hold it up.

I'm not the only one beaming at the sight of him. Even the stone-faced Sin cracks a smile, albeit a very small one. It creases his face enough that I peg him to be about sixty, which makes me wonder if he's looking at the facility for his mother or possibly his wife.

"This is Mr. Whiskers."

"Your stuffed animal?" Sin's studious eyes move from it to me, the intensity of his gaze so much harsher than is warranted by my crazy talk.

Unnerved, I take in a breath. "Mr. Whiskers is so much more than that. He's a therapy stuffed animal. You can even pop him in the microwave to warm him up."

I avoid talking about my past or that Mr. Whiskers has been my personal security blanket for nearly twenty years.

Sin nods. "Do all residents get a toy? Or just the bad ones?" His contempt doesn't bother me. He doesn't understand, and it's my job to help him understand.

"Sparrow Wellness and Assisted Living is unlike any facility you may have seen. Our occupants range in age from twenty to eighty-two. Sometimes, a little non-threatening toy is a great way for people to open up. I didn't have to say a word about him, and you asked."

His face is stone. No hint as to whether he's annoyed or amused. His eyes wander through the opening to a vacant room. "Continue."

"Even if they aren't interested in a little support from a cuddly friend, he's a big hit with the children who visit. We keep a small stockpile in the back."

"Trauma victims?" He mutters the question under his breath in a way that sounds less like distaste and more like hope.

"We cater to a wide range of conditions, trauma being just one of them. Some residents have degenerative conditions that require more care than their families can provide. Others don't have families, in which case we become their family if their physician recommends us."

Sin takes several steps into the room, moving his gaze from the warm cream walls and big bay window to me. "Looking for a family, Ms. Palmer?"

His tone is sharp and icy, with enough condescension that I have to remind myself that people in pain tend to inflict pain. He's just hurting, and I'm the closest target within striking distance. But it's not directed at me. *Even if it is the truth.*

"Just looking to help as many people as I can." I hold my smile as I step away, shooing off a flurry of emotions that I'll need to deal with later. For now, Sin is in his role of distrustful client. It's up to me to win him over.

His brisk footsteps close in quickly from behind.

We stop at the courtyard, where a few residents have opted to spend their morning lounging on lawn furniture, enjoying the sun. We walk in silence. He takes an interest in a resident, Angie, lost in the strokes of a painting she's creating. I use the time to take a closer look at his paperwork, only now noticing he's left several areas blank.

It's not uncommon. People tend to be guarded their first time walking through. It's a long way from *nice to meet you* to *I trust you with my loved one*, but it's a familiar road I've traveled many, many times.

"It's you," Sin says, and I look up.

Seeing the painting this close, I realize the resemblance is uncanny. I'd almost believe it was me if not for the elegance of the off-the-shoulder gown Angie has painted her in, or the delight in her eyes that could never radiate from mine. It's how I want to look. Confident. Complete. Happy. Instead, my heart is riddled with so many holes, half the time it feels like it's about to collapse under all the damage.

Taking a closer look, I see the white curl in her subject's curly black hair—identical to the one that inexplicably grows at my right temple. Angie nods, beaming with a grin as she silently lets me know it is me.

It's a version of me that could only happen in Angie's beautiful imagination.

Grateful, I hug Angie, being gentle to avoid overdoing it. Her muscles are weak. Every word from her lips is a fight, but they're always worth waiting for. Especially today as she sounds out two words.

"H-h-hap-p-py b-b-b-irth-d-day."

My heart leaps as she completes the short sentence. It's the most she's said in a week, and I find myself speechless, if not a bit teary-eyed.

"Sorry, do you mind if I steal Ivy for a second?"

Derrick interrupts, probably to keep me from outright blubbering. He's more than my boss, though no one would know it. We've been a couple for nearly a year but keeping our relationship under wraps was his idea as much as mine. Sort of.

I keep one eye on Sin, watching as he carries on a one-sided conversation with Angie. He doesn't seem concerned that she isn't responding. On the contrary, his smile is genuine, even though he receives nothing more than a few polite nods back. But I'm ready to jump in if he demands any more.

Derrick's hands stay pocketed, the way they always do when he's hiding something. Maybe it's a surprise. Like dinner at a fancy restaurant on the waterfront. Or cuddling together in front of a romantic bonfire on the beach.

Between his work schedule and mine—which is a result of his—it's been weeks since I've had any action. I'm bursting at the seams with sexual frustration, so if my birthday celebration is a beer, a grilled cheese, and twenty solid minutes of hitting it hard during whatever sci-fi show he can't live without, I'll take it.

I'm grinning like an idiot when he says low, "I really need you to bring this one home, babe. Seal the deal. The numbers need to look good. I've got a big meeting tonight."

"Tonight? But—"

His cell phone buzzes, and he takes it, mouthing, "Gotta go," as he winks and rushes back inside.

"Why are you in this, Ms. Palmer?" Sin asks as he sidles up to me.

"What?" I scoop my jaw up off the ground, realizing he isn't referring to my conversation with Derrick.

Sin means my work. Of course, he does. His thousand-yard stare roves across the lush grounds, taking it in while not focusing on anything at all.

"The same reason everyone works here. It's personal. We've all been here. Helping family members who need assistance."

He turns, narrowing his eyes. "Family?" The way he says the word is strained, as if he doesn't believe me.

It compels me to share more than I normally would. "My mother had a degenerative condition. There was a lot of pain in her last years of life. I did all I could."

I don't talk about the specifics. How by the time a doctor diagnosed her liver disease, nothing could be done. That it never stopped her from the drugs or the alcohol. Or that despite the unbearable pain she suffered every second of her last days of life, she pushed me away until she was too weak or too tired to put up a fight. There's no way I can explain how you can love a person with all your heart when they seem to hate you with all of theirs, so I don't try.

By the look on Sin's face, I've already given him an uncomfortable amount of information to unpack. So, I wrap it up, quickly finishing. "I did what I could to make her comfortable."

The hard lines of his face soften. "I'm sorry for what you've been through."

"Thank you." The practiced smile I use in times like these emerge, and I nod appreciatively, steering our discussion back where it belongs. On him. And not because Derrick wants me to close the deal, but because this man and his family need me. And that's why I'm here.

"The first steps are never easy," I say as a gentle reminder. "We have different levels of care and service. Can you tell me more about the person who brought you here today?"

He spends another moment looking me up and down, torment storming behind his eyes as they finally settle on mine.

I don't know what to make of it, but situations like these can be delicate. With all my encounters, I'm patient as I let the client drive the discussion, deciding for themselves if they'll tear the bandage off bit by bit, or rip it off all at once.

With an abrupt huff, he steps away, his large, determined strides taking him inside the facility and back toward the lobby. I rush after him, but don't shout out his name or make a scene, not wanting to draw attention from the residents or staff . . . especially Derrick.

Sin wastes no time depositing his visitor badge on the desk, and I nearly break into a jog to catch up to his mile-long stride. When he bolts out the front doors, I'm right behind him, struggling to catch my breath.

"Sin," I say, winded but compassionate. He stops but doesn't face me. "If I've said anything—"

"You haven't."

His reply is so matter-of-fact, I feel silly for suggesting it. So, I reclaim my smile, if only for my own benefit.

"I know trust takes time. My card," I say, holding it out and feeling doubly foolish when he doesn't take it.

Instead, he sneers.

This is the point where others might give up, but I don't. It's the people who push you off the most that are in the most pain. At least, that's the excuse I've always given myself.

He eyes the card, then casts an amused glance to the sky. After an awkward second of silent conversation between him and a few puffy white clouds, he faces me. The hand he places on my shoulder feels paternal. "I don't need your card, Ms. Palmer. The person who brought me here today was you."

Unbuttoning his blazer, he fishes a thin envelope from the inside pocket and hands it to me as a dark car with tinted windows pulls up beside him. "Someone recently told me the first steps are never easy, Ms. Palmer."

A well-dressed chauffeur rushes around to open the back door, and as soon as Sin is seated inside, the man returns to the driver's seat.

The darkened window rolls down, and Sin's smile widens. "Happy birthday."

He slides on a pair of sunglasses as the car rolls away.

CHAPTER 2

Ivy

THE BLACK TOWN car makes a left at the end of the drive, disappearing behind a thicket of birch trees, and I'm left there scratching my head. What just happened? I take another look at the plain white envelope in my hand, ready to open it until I notice Derrick. He's been watching from the large window of his office, a practice of his I've come to accept.

There's an intensity to his expression, one I meet with a cheerful smile. It takes him a moment before he returns it, waving me over. Maybe there's a surprise waiting for me. Like gathering the staff over to sing "Happy Birthday." Or an intimate cupcake with a single candle for me to wish upon.

"Everything all right?" Derrick asks as I enter. It's just him and me and the ever-growing clusters of paperwork and folders covering his desk. My hopes for a cupcake are instantly dashed, and it's a wonder he can find anything in the small space. For every new meeting with his accountant, the mounds of paperwork are only getting worse. He closes in from behind me, though the door remains open.

"Yes. He's going to think it over," I say as I slip the envelope into the roomy pocket of my cardigan. I want to remind him that sales aren't made in a day. That trust must be earned. But the irony is enough for me to bite my tongue.

I should tell Derrick about the envelope. For once, trust him. Really let him in. It feels self-sabotaging not to.

As often as I repeat the usual mantra, *I should trust him,* over and over again in my head, I can't deny the parts of my mind and heart that don't . . . and it's not for a lack of trying. Or admitting to myself that I'm damaged goods, the byproduct of an absentee mother and father unknown.

But Derrick is my ticket to a normal relationship, even if things between us have felt a bit uncomfortable lately. It's just a hiccup, one every couple encounters. He's stable. Sweet. A bit of a workaholic, which means I haven't seen him much in the past three weeks. But at least he has a J-O-B, and that should count for something, right?

Still, I can't help but shove the envelope deeper into my oversized pocket, hiding it from both my boyfriend and my boss. No matter how hard I try, distrust slithers between us, threatening to pry us apart.

Let's face it, I have issues, and trust is just the tip of the iceberg.

One of his arms wraps around me. Instead of giving him the usual elbow to the ribs, I nuzzle into him, and it feels . . . nice. Warm and caring and . . . nice. That is, until he releases me. And just like that, I second-guess everything.

Am I like Goldilocks complaining that my man is too nice?

Derrick's shirt is perfectly fitted, the navy blue tapering over his chest and abs before disappearing into his slacks. It looks professional and sexy, though I still prefer his lucky polo. His sweet superstition is that whenever he wears it, luck lands in his lap. As if I was a manifestation of luck.

"Chase another one off?" he says, only half-teasing me.

With his half smile and adorable gaze, maybe he's ready to finally make it official. "Aren't you afraid someone will see us?" I playfully ask, wondering if we can finally stop hiding our status from coworkers and Facebook alike. Be a couple in the actual light of day.

I know I agreed to keep our relationship under wraps, but maybe this is a baby step in the right direction. Hope blooms from deep within my chest that maybe, just maybe, I'm finally learning to trust.

"You're probably right," he says, pulling away to bring us back to a proper boss-employee distance apart. When my frown catches his eye, he lowers his voice. "Hey, it's not forever. Just for now. Meeting you was my destiny."

His sweet words and wink revive my smile, but before I can slip him a kiss, he steps back.

Noticing the envelope, he asks, "What's that?"

It would be so easy to tell him about the tour with Sin. The strange encounter and Sin's bizarre escape. Why can't I take the envelope out and open it with Derrick? Share something, *anything*, with my boyfriend of nearly a year.

I slide the unmarked envelope from my pocket, flipping it aimlessly. "Just a letter."

"I'm running to the post office after work, then I've got a meeting. Need me to mail it for you?"

"I've got it," I say, forcing a smile. "Meeting?" On my birthday?

Derrick has taken several meetings this week away from the office. And another dinner meeting? This can't be good.

His nod is reluctant, and I know when to back off. But I offer him all the support he needs, cuddling Mr. Whiskers against his neck. And like Sin before him, Derrick can't help but crack a smile.

"You and that . . . cat."

I don't know what word he mentally used to fill in the blank between *that* and *cat*, and I don't care. I'm tired of being ruled by my stupid doubts. And they are stupid.

But I tuck Mr. Whiskers back into my pocket, leaning closer to Derrick's rigid stance. "I need something for luck. I mean, we can't all have a lucky polo."

CHAPTER 3
Ivy

"Table for two. Under Brooke Everly," my best friend says, rescuing me from a birthday dinner for one of mac and cheese.

"You reserved a table?" I ask as we're seated, surprised because we never get a table. We always sit at the bar.

"The strongest they have . . . so we can dance on it. It's your birthday!" She squeals loud enough that absolutely everyone is looking. "And just because your boyfriend has to work doesn't mean we celebrate less. After this, it's karaoke time."

Her elbow nudges mine, and I know she's serious. My throat dangerously tight, I choke down the ball of fear with a few sips of the chilled water our waiter has placed in front of me.

Brooke instantly demands two tequilas. Both for her. "And keep them coming," she tells the waiter.

We've plowed through our first basket of chips as she tosses back her second shot.

"So, let me get this straight," Brooke says as she taps her lip with her index finger. "Some mysterious good-looking guy books a tour with you just to deliver mail and check out your ass?" She slurs the word *ass* and motions for the waiter. "Tell me he at least offered you a lap dance."

"He did not."

"Fucker. So, what did the letter say?"

I shrug. "It's still in my pocket. I got busy, and—"

Her eyes widen. "You didn't want to open it in front of Derrick in case it's a dick pic."

I deadpan. "Who would print out a dick pic?"

"A man who fills the page. You can't open it until after dinner. Birthday present number one."

Laughing, I shrug and dunk another chip into hot, gooey cheese. "Good-looking, yes. But more than twice my age, at least. And we all know twice my age is my hard limit."

"Really? I'll bet he's still hotter than Derrick. You rarely spend the night at his place, and we both know he's never at yours. Plus, he never takes you out. Ever. What kind of eighty-year-old boyfriend is he?"

"For your information, he's thirty. And I'm trying to be supportive as he builds his career."

"For a year? And when's the last time you've had sex?" she shouts, trying to be heard above the lively Mexican music.

Our waiter refills my water, grinning broadly. Sweltering heat rises up my face as I melt into the seat and die of embarrassment. Brooke roars with laughter, planting herself facedown along the bench.

"This coming from a woman whose face is kissing an area where someone's ass has been. After they've eaten their weight in Mexican food."

I ball up my napkin and toss it at my drunk friend's head, which does little good. If anything, it eggs her on, as she moves on from laughter to a perfect whale-song combination of howling, raucous heaving, and silent squeals.

She rubs the flood of hysterical tears from her face before pointing a finger straight up, conveying how she needs a moment to catch her breath.

Hushed, I lean over. "I've had sex," I say, arguing with the giddy drunk girl. "For your information, I have it regularly."

"Like as regularly as when the salmon swim upstream?"

The waiter brings our food—two shrimp quesadillas for me and a taco salad the size of my Honda Civic for Brooke. I glare at her over the rim of my water glass as she orders a margarita.

"Virgin?" she shouts, having lost all control over the volume of her voice.

I scowl at her until I realize she was talking about a drink. Which actually sounds good.

Turning to the waiter, I ask, "Can you do a pineapple margarita with no alcohol?"

He nods and heads off.

"And more nachos," Brooke hollers after him.

In an instant, her elated happy face drops. Despite the fact that she's a champion lush who can usually out-shot or out-chug any man, I'm almost afraid she's about to be sick.

"You okay?" I ask, ready to rush her to the ladies' room.

She merely points past me, and I turn to see whatever zapped every last drop of happy-go-lucky from her face.

Lo and behold, it's Derrick.

I'm elated that he made it to my birthday celebration after

all, until I see he's not in the professional button-down shirt he was wearing earlier at work. And he's not alone.

This version of Derrick looks freshly showered, his hair still damp and curled in a pretty-boy style that actually makes him look younger. Wearing his faded jeans that are my favorite, he's seated at the bar, relaxed as his spread-eagle legs give easy access to let a sloppy blonde slide in between them. She's made herself perfectly comfortable, smoothing her fingers against his chest and shoulders and pretty much all over his lucky fucking polo.

I square my shoulders, and before I know it, I've crossed the length of room, vaguely aware of Brooke huffing, "Shit," as her footsteps stumble behind me. I'm seconds from yanking the blonde by the hair—southern style—when I come to my senses and realize it's not her I'm pissed at.

"Oh, fuck," Derrick says like a dumbass because that's what he is. A worthless, dickless dumbass. He fumbles his way from behind the body of a woman whose perfume smells way too familiar because, like the man she's draped all over, that's also mine.

"Is 'oh, fuck' all you have to say? I guess she's your destiny, too." I frantically search the bar for the biggest drink within reach to toss in his face.

"What's going on?"

When his companion turns to face me, I realize it's none other than his accountant. Which explains all those closed-door and after-work meetings.

"Hey. Iris, right?" she says with the charm of a pole dancer, and now I'm searching the bar for two of the biggest drinks I can find—preferably crammed full of ice.

"Don't make a scene, Ivy," Derrick says calmly like a total idiot. "We're hardly exclusive."

"Excuse me? You're the one who was talking marriage and kids. You're the one who's always asking what cut of diamond I prefer and where our honeymoon should be."

His lips tighten, and his words come out cool. "You can't pin this on me. I need passion. Spontaneity. A woman who will throw caution to the wind. The most I got out of you was your toothbrush."

He means a girl who will throw condoms to the wind. "And that's my fault? You're the one who wanted to keep our relationship on the down-low, and now I know why."

"Grow up. You don't want exclusive. You want to roam fast and free and with whatever guy rolls up. Like Limo-man this afternoon. What was in that envelope he gave you? Cash? A hotel room key?"

"What the fuck, Derrick? No."

At least, I don't think so. Besides, Derrick's so-called accountant is two seconds from sucking him off at the bar, so why am I the one on trial?

Derrick crosses his arms over his chest. "Yeah? Prove it."

He casts an arrogant glance at the pocket of my cardigan because, unlike him, I didn't have time to shower and change clothes before going out. I was actually working.

"I have nothing to prove." Which now looks like I have everything to prove. *Dammit.*

When I feel a tug at the envelope, I whirl around.

Brooke waves Exhibit A suggestively in the air. "And what if she hasn't been cheating on your sorry ass, Dare-dick? What are you willing to wager?"

At least my ride-or-die has my back, though I feel a bead of perspiration trail down the nape of my neck at her suggestion. And since there's no backing down now, I square my shoulders and pray to God that Derrick is wrong.

Derrick waves her off. "It's not like you didn't already destroy the evidence."

"It's still sealed," I say, not certain if I'm making the situation better or worse but not willing to let my friend hang in the wind.

His expression sours. "Fine. What do you want if I'm wrong?"

"Your fucking car, jackass," Brooke says.

Wow. Her balls get all kinds of big after that much tequila. And when my bestie dives in headfirst, demanding his shiny new Mercedes convertible, there's only one thing to say.

"Yeah, Dare-dick," I say, repeating her insult because it's kind of catchy and totally spot-on as he plays fast and loose with Sluts-R-Us over here.

That's not jealousy talking. That's his accountant's cherry red lips now printing a path up another guy's neck before her tongue lands in his ear. It sickens me to remember that you've had sex with everyone your partner's had sex with. Perhaps a few weeks of no action with Derrick is just enough time to avoid a collision course with a round of STDs.

"Fine," he says, bellying up and stepping into my space. I anchor myself in place, ready for whatever he's got. Until he says, "Then if I win, you quit."

"Quit?" I squeak out.

I can't quit. What I do isn't just a job. It's my life. For years, I've cared for every single person in the center. Working evenings. Weekends. Christmas fucking morning. And now he wants me to quit?

Derrick is going too far. I'm not quitting my job over a stupid bet or even a breakup. No way. Not a chance.

I'm about to tell him so when Brooke cracks open the seal of the envelope and pulls out an old-looking photograph. Who in the world has photos anymore?

She flips it around and trombones the square to and from her face in the booze-filled hope of reading it. "Who's Olivia?"

"What?" Carefully, I take the delicate photo from her hand, staring at it hard, as hard as I can. My heart pounds wildly against my ribs, and I stand there, stunned. I blink before I regain my senses and can move.

Brooke slaps the empty envelope on Derrick's chest. "Ivy doesn't need your job. She's an overqualified badass who's tired of taking your shit."

Oh. My. God. Brooke really needs to stop talking now.

"Fuck both of you," Derrick spits out. "I'm not giving you my car."

As Derrick storms off, Brooke shouts after him, "Way to be a bad loser, Dare-dick."

It isn't until she wipes my cheek that I realize I'm crying.

"Hey, don't cry. He doesn't deserve you," she says, stroking my hair.

"It's not that," I say, staring at the image of my mother. At least, I think it's my mother. It's as if Angie's magic wand has brushed alchemist strokes across her image. Her dark curls are thick and full, framing round cherub cheeks and a big, beautiful smile I've never seen her wear. I almost didn't recognize her.

Next to her stands a man I don't know. His dark wavy hair is the perfect crown to his tall stature and confident stance. His lips are a line that barely tips up, and his dimpled chin could have been molded to form mine. But it's his eyes that draw me in. Instantly I want to know him, and it bothers me that I don't.

On the back is a riddle, one I reread again and again . . . and again.

For
Olivia Ann Palmer.

"What is it?" Brooke asks with a side hug that wraps me tight and squeezes out my reply.

"It's me. I'm Olivia Ann Palmer."

Ready for more? Check out SINS of the Syndicate, Book 1 in the SINS Series today!

>> **SINS of the Syndicate**
SINS & Ivy
SINS: The Debt

SINS: The Deal (Book 1 in Enzo's Trilogy)
SINS & Lies (Book 2 in Enzo's Trilogy)
SINS & Temptation (Book 3 in Enzo's Trilogy)

Marked

BOYS OF BISHOP MOUNTAIN

CHAPTER 1

Jess

HAVE you ever believed that if you wished for something hard enough, you could make it happen?

I did. It all started when my mom used to say, "Never underestimate the power of a wish." Then she'd hold the fluffy-white dandelion in front of me as my cheeks puffed with air. "Blow, baby girl!"

And I would. Wasting a universe of wishes with reckless abandon on books, candy, and toys. It's like slots for toddlers: The more you wish, the more chances you have of one of those wishes coming true.

It took a few years before I got serious. Doubled-down on just one wish. What was it Hannibal Lecter said? We covet what we see every day? Who knew the words of a fictional psychopath could ring so true?

And see Mark Donovan, I did.

My brother's best friend. Yeah, try not seeing him. Dark, carefree waves that melted down to eyes that changed with his mood. Golden caramel at his happiest. Moody winter green when he was brooding.

He was it. My first big wish. My first epic fail.

Every night for a month, I wished I would grow up to marry him. And then I did the unthinkable. With my little-girl outside voice, I said it. "I am going to marry you." Said it straight to his beautiful boy face.

Considering I was six and he was twelve, it went over like a loud fart in a packed church. What started with a wince morphed into uncontrollable laughter, culminating in Mark doubling over on the floor.

Oh, that last part wasn't from laughter. It was from my angry little-girl fist jabbing a full-force punch square at his balls.

This cautionary tale taught me two things. First, boys apparently can't breathe without their balls. And second, wishes aren't meant to be trite or trivial. If only a few wishes are meant to come true, make each one precious. Make them count.

When my dear, sweet parents made their way to heaven—a pain so raw, it hurt just to breathe—I had faith. For every dandelion I plucked, I wished messages could make their way up through the clouds, delivered by the wind.

I wished Nana Winnie was as happy as a lark, cutting out crazy patterns for her latest quilt. I wished our old Labrador retriever, Saint, was with them, running fast and free to catch a Frisbee from my dad. I wished every time I sang to the clouds, my mom could feel the love I poured into every note. Knew how much I missed her. Missed them all.

When my brothers moved away, lured by the military, I

wished them back. Brian showed up the next day, the Rock of Gibraltar by my side ever since.

How? I have no idea. Considering he's a sniper at the beck and call of the Army, I can't imagine how he worked that out. But we both knew it couldn't last forever, and the lifeline he cast me was beginning to strain.

In five short days, he returns to the other side of the world, and the last thing he needs to worry about is me.

So, today's dandelion is for a job. Not just any job. Just a small promotion that keeps the lights on and cements me in place, home on Bishop Mountain.

On my day off, and armed with the fluffiest dandelion I could find, I close my eyes and imagine my mom holding it out. My small smile makes way to a gust of breath. I blow all my fears and doubts away, letting the feather-soft wisps fly free on a breeze.

One wish. One shot. And one man who can make it all happen.

CHAPTER 2
Jess

"Have you seen Tyler?" I ask, standing a respectable distance from the customer side of the bar.

Anita frowns as she side-eyes me while flipping a shaker with finesse. "I thought you were off."

I shrug. "I am." Though I have no idea why. I pause for a beat. "But I wanted to pick up my check." I can't help my envious stare at her nametag. Anita Mae, Bartender.

She nods, her smile knowing. "And call dibs on my job?"

I scrunch up my face. "Too obvious?"

"Uh, it's called initiative. You're a Bishop. I'd expect nothing less." She notices the space I've created between me and the bar. Bartending in the great state of New York at eighteen? Totally legit. Taste-testing even one drop of alcohol? Not so much.

And as I am the last of the Bishop children to work in this establishment, let's just say I don't want to be the one to eff it all up with the liquor authority.

"You're not a kid anymore, Jess. Step on up!"

Proudly, I do. With a lighter, she demonstrates a technique called *flaming an orange peel*. With the strike of a match and the flick of her fingers, a fireball showers the drink, then vanishes behind a small trail of smoke.

"Doesn't that burn?" I ask.

She shakes her head. "You're not really lighting the peel as much as spraying the orange oil against the flame into the glass." She walks me slowly through the motions. "See?"

I nod. Rumor is, her promotion is in the bag, which leaves her job up for grabs. It's a long shot, but I've been practicing. Thank God for YouTube.

She peers over thick-framed glasses. "Master this trick. People eat it up, and the tips flow like water." She gestures grandly to the wall of liquor and art-deco accents. "This will all be yours someday."

Fascinated, I glance around. "There's so much to learn."

She tosses a small notebook on the glossy wood. "Here. You want the job? Memorize this."

Flipping through, I realize it has to be fifty pages of customized cocktails from the *Adirondack Sunset* to *Donovan's Deadly Twist*. But when my gaze hits *Bishop's Breeze*, I pause, and my eyes well up. I expected it to be a drink created by Brian, Rex, or Cade—any one of my brothers—but it's not. It was written by Henry.

Henry James Bishop, my father. My fingers skim across the page as I inhale pride and exhale sadness. Vodka. Lemon. Honey. Club soda with a splash of Moscato. I choke up. I can almost see him making it for mom.

Anita's warm hand covers mine. "Anything I can do?"

Rewind time. Stop them from getting in that car.

"No," I say softly. *Not unless you can bring my parents back.* It takes a breath before the pain subsides and a few blinks to dislodge an annoyingly stubborn tear.

"Lunch?" she says kindly.

I decline with a hopeful grin. "Rain check?" Considering I'm blowing all my money on my gift for Brian, I will absolutely take a free lunch IOU.

Sharp, jabbing pains erupt in the lowest point of my gut. *Not now.* I suck in a breath to stave it off. A hard pinch comes again, a tight twist. I hug both arms against my belly, wrestling the pain away, grateful that Anita's too busy to notice.

"Hmm . . ." She fills a thick glass mug with whatever's on tap. "Tyler?"

She thinks for a moment while I try not to double over in pain. Or cry out "*Mercy*" to the gods of pain.

Month after month, my periods are ten times worse, and over-the-counter medications are barely making a dent. With any luck, the extra-extra-strength medication I got at the drugstore will kick in any second now.

While I bite my lip like a bullet, Anita ponders on. "Tyler . . ."

Maybe it's the repeated knife jabs to the gut talking, but if one more person says they haven't seen Tyler Donovan, I'll throw down like a toddler. I'm two seconds from unceremoniously face-planting onto the questionably clean floor, arms and legs flailing about in full-on meltdown mode.

Anita sets a pink-and-purple drink at the pickup station and a mug of beer next to it before sliding her glasses to the tip of her nose.

"So, you have to see Tyler?" she sings suggestively. Or hopefully. I swear, the woman is vying for the official title of Cupid.

The knife jab below the belly subsides to a dull ache enough for me to play along. "Obviously, because Tyler knows how to make a girl truly happy."

She gives me the hairy eyeball. "You're lucky you're legal," she says, smirking as she waggles her brows.

"All I need is a few minutes alone with him. Just me and Tyler so he can"—I deadpan— "pay me." I lower my voice and clasp my hands in prayer. "And pitch him a dozen reasons for why I'd be perfect for your job."

By her outrageous yawn, she's underwhelmed. "Boring." She leans in confidentially. "Moment of truth . . . which one?"

"Which one what?"

"Which one of the Donovans melts your butter?"

Which? How can she ask me that? I mean, they're all friends with my brothers. *Which* makes it weird.

Wide-eyed, Anita smiles expectantly as I think it through. Anything to take my mind off the pain, though it's eased up enough that I'm no longer tasting blood from my lower lip.

Ignoring my childhood faux pas of a wish, I run through the list.

There's Tyler, who's inherently sexy because he has my paycheck. He's the older, wiser, kinder of the Donovan brothers. His sandy-blond waves are always as carefree as his soul, and his twenty-seven-year-old smile warms you from the inside out. One day in the not-too-distant future, this business will be his kingdom, an attractive quality that the vagina of every eligible bachelorette in the tri-county region has zeroed in on.

Hunk-worthiness? A ten and a half. On the date-worthy

scale, I can't even go there. He's almost paternal. Or a really hot uncle you hope will find his forever match. Whenever I come in, he's always checking to see how I'm doing and if I've eaten. Thanks to this place, I have.

Then there's Zac, the youngest and three years older than me. A young McDreamy in his own right; his looks are totally wasted. The man has been my BFF since forever ago, but he never dates. Between studying at New York University and launching his own mogul career, you'd think the man was thirty-one, not twenty-one.

Over summers and holiday breaks, he returns to Saratoga Springs to shake things up. Moving the inventory system from the caveman era into the next millennium. Shifting the ordering to the cloud and ensuring it takes everything from Venmo to Bitcoin. And launching a spruced-up website with candid shots that always manage to blow up Instagram, which he often credits me for.

Every chance I get, I snap outrageous photos and videos, and at Zac's insistence, they've posted every single one. Food photos. Tyler clowning around, serving a bachelorette party in nothing but a black apron. Well, he had shorts on, but you couldn't tell from the front. Even simple things like Anita plopping dry ice into drinks at Halloween.

Zac says I have raw talent. I call it an obsession with Mrs. D.'s food.

Zac will forever be my biggest cheerleader and best friend, but something more? Let's just say our one and only test-the-waters kiss was all we needed to be eternally friend-zoned. Plus, I'm not sure he'll ever settle down. Core-of-the-Earth-level hotness? A thousand percent. A compulsive workaholic? Ten-thousand percent.

And last, but not least, there's Mark. The very same Marcus Evan Donavon my child mind thought I could marry. Silly girl. I couldn't possibly marry an ass, and make no mistake, that man is an ass.

As if reading my thoughts, Anita asks, "Ooh, is it Mark?"

Heat flares up my neck to my cheeks as I scoff. "Mark? Mark hates me."

"He does not."

"He even gave me that stupid nickname."

Anita coos at me. "It's adorable."

My palm is affronted before I am, and it flies in her face. "Don't even."

Her hands raise in surrender as she smartly backs up a step. "Okay, okay. Just saying, he's not terrible on the eyes."

When Anita gets googly-eyed for Mark, I gag. She grabs a ticket and pulls a highball from the shelf to work on her next drink.

All I can think is...Mark? Really?

I mean, to look at, yes. Agreed. If Mark had a mute button, he'd be the perfect man. The problem with him—or rather, the biggest problem with him—is that his looks far overshadow his tiny, little pea-brain. That and his two-sizes too-small heart.

Have you ever seen a man too beautiful to exist? Sure, in and of itself, it's not a reason to hate him. What I hate is that Mark wields it like a weapon. Whenever he walks into a room, I feel the need to dispense chastity belts with reckless abandon.

Again, I'm not talking about your garden-variety good looks, as in he looks great in a pair of jeans with an insta-swoon dimple that could launch a thousand ships. I'm talking about a legs-locked, knees-weak, heart-stopping level of sex appeal that would stand out in a sea of Hemsworths. The irony is that with all that heat, Mark is too cold.

Anita pops the cork on a bottle of Moscato and works on a Bellini. "Well, if your heart's set on Tyler or Zac, you're SOL. I just remembered that Tyler isn't here. He and Zac went fishing with their dad before Zac returns to school."

I nibble my lower lip again, worry twisting my gut.

"Nope. Don't do that," Anita says, frowning.

"Huh? Do what?"

She waves an accusatory strawberry-margarita painted fingernail in my face. "That thing where your brows pinch so hard, they nearly touch. Trust me, you're too young to start with the permanent angry line." She wipes down the bar. "You worried about Brian leaving?"

"No," I lie, lifting a defiant chin. "Brian has been here long enough. Having him take care of me since my parents—"

My mouth dries, sand filling my throat before I can say the words. I breathe through it until words come out.

"Anyway, the military gave him all the leave they could. I'm an adult. I've graduated. I'm a big girl, and my brother's a big boy. We can take care of ourselves." I say this out loud at least a dozen times a day, because any day now, I'll believe it.

Anita places a bowl of mixed nuts between us and pops a few into her mouth. "Then what is it?"

Deflated, I sigh. "I have five days to get Brian his going-away gift before his deployment."

"That should be plenty of time."

"I need to be able to afford it first. It costs my entire paycheck."

She lifts a brow. "All of your paycheck?"

I nod. "Along with the engraving, yes. I caught him drooling at the jewelers over some stupid-expensive tactical watch. After an insane amount of searching, I found a pre-owned one, but I have to pick it up today. The owner already has other buyers." I'm about to show her on my phone, but my battery's already low, and I still need to use it to find this guy. Wiggling my fingers at her, I say, "Give me your phone."

Anita hands it to me, and I pull up the Laney Jewelers website, then scroll to the right photo. With a two-toned whistle, she approves.

I smile. "And then hopefully, I'll have time to get it engraved before Brian leaves."

"You mean Brian and Mark. What, no gift for his bestie?" she teases.

My lips quirk as my narrowed eyes respond for me.

"Hey, if push comes to shove, girl, I've got you." She holds up a paring knife. "Seriously, how hard can it be to scratch two Bs on the metal band?"

"What I had in mind is a little more than his initials, and this watch is worth weeks of my life," I say indignantly as I lower her knife-wielding hand. "As skilled as you are with slicing and dicing, how about we leave the pretty letter carving to the experts." I tap the counter, not sure what to do. "Who can I get my check from?"

"You can get it from Mark."

"What? Mark's here?" My brows pop up as the name of my

arch-nemesis rings through the air. Or is it just nemesis? "Mark never comes here. And why isn't he fishing with everyone else?"

Smiling, she shrugs. "Mrs. D.'s working out the details for the Whitney wedding. I guess he's filling in."

"Perfect." I let out a frustrated sigh. "Any idea where he is?" Anita shakes her head as I slide off the leather stool. "I guess I'll stop looking for Tyler and hunt down Mark."

"Hang on." She fishes cash from the tip jar and hands it to me.

Blinking, I stare at her. "What's this?"

Her hands grab mine, shoving the bills into it. "A bunch of tourists went all out at brunch. Take it. I don't want you not to have a paycheck. You'll be working this side of the bar soon enough."

Emotions overwhelm me as I stare down at the twenties, tens, and fives. This isn't just how Anita is. It's how everyone is here. Always looking out for me when I suspect it least and need it most. Everyone here cares for me. In return, I have to care for them back.

Counting it quickly, I split it right down the middle and toss half back in the jar. "Thanks," I say, rushing out of there before I'm a blubbering puddle in the middle of the floor.

Sternly, I wipe my cheeks and make my way down the hall. I can cry when I'm at home. That's what showers are for.

Scowling, I mutter under my breath. "Yoo-hoo . . . Satan. Come out, come out, wherever you are."

Where Tyler and Zac are wholesome goodness wrapped up in sunshine and smiles, Mark is the polar opposite, ready to fight, run, or fornicate at a moment's notice. His brothers are easygoing sails on tranquil waters, while Mark is a storm.

And those eyes. Shamefully, I've stared at them more than once.

Some men were meant to build castles while others were born to slay dragons. That's Mark. A hot-blooded fighting machine who can't turn it off. It's what makes him the best. And the broodiest.

When Brian entered the Army, Mark rushed in after him, besties since their stupid blood oath in the fifth grade. Seriously, how deep did they need to cut? They both required five stitches each. But that was them. Two beautiful idiots pridefully counting every last scar.

It's the reason why no matter how hard I try, I can't avoid Mark. Like my brother's shadow, he's always around. A personal tormentor, ready and eager to strike at will.

I pop my head into the break room. A few waitresses are eating a late lunch and gossiping about customers.

Gasping, Kara looks up at me. "I thought you were off," she says, offended at my very presence. "Tyler said you needed a personal day." Her eyes roll to a resentful stop. "Must be nice."

Why would Tyler tell them that? I ignore her, and not just because Kara's an ass, but because convincing Kara that Tyler is wrong would be as fruitful as convincing Mark I should be a bartender. There's no point. It'll never happen. But I still need to pick up my check. "Have either of you seen Mark?"

"Oh my God," Starr says as she whips back her pink hair. "Is Mark *Danger Zone* Donovan here?"

Kara claps and squeals like a seal, while I rub my temple, praying that the migraine she just spurred up goes away. High-pitched and hopeless, she carries on. "He's so lickable. I heard he now holds the record for the most confirmed kills."

Confused, I stare. "How does that make him hot?"

She smirks. "You wouldn't understand." She scans me up and down before dismissing me with her eyes. "You're too young."

"I'm only a year younger than you, Kara."

She scoops her breasts into her crossed arms, forcing cleavage that even her overstuffed push-up couldn't tackle. "There's a world of difference in a year."

Perhaps to a dog.

"Trust me," Starr says. "His brothers are princes, but Mark Donovan is a full-fledged demi-god." She licks her spoon suggestively. "I've got something that sharpshooter can aim at."

She sucks her finger, amplifying the point. I dry heave and leave the room. Only God knows where that finger's been.

Kara calls after me. "Tell him we're looking for him, too, okay?"

Their giggles echo wildly as I shake my head. *Sure. Why not? Because maybe if I offer two semi-virginal sacrifices to your demi-God, he'll give me that promotion I desperately need.*

"Jess?" I hear Mark say. His deep, gravelly voice flows effortlessly down the hall, though I don't see him.

As I approach his office, the door is ajar. I slide a hand on the handle, pausing as soon as I hear, "What about her?" Because Mark isn't talking to me, he's talking *about* me.

The door is cracked ever so slightly, an obvious invitation to listen in. His heavy footsteps move farther away, and I nudge the door a hair, wide enough to peer inside.

Framed by the large picture window at the other end of the office, Beelzebub stands in all his glory: dark blue jeans, crisp white shirt, and chestnut-brown hair mussed to perfection. The million-mile stare he sports is fixed somewhere off in the distance as he presses the cell phone to his ear.

It's wrong of me to stare. But I can't not stare. I mean, it's hardly the first time I've seen Mark Donovan. It's just the first time I've dared to unapologetically stare at his ass.

He shifts in place, and the move is hypnotic. Did he bulk up ... his butt?

I knew he did some heavy lifting, but this is ridiculous. I mean, once, when traffic was blocked, he and Brian lifted a fallen maple to the side of the road. By themselves. So, yeah, I get it. Muscle mayhem. But now, his arm bulge alone has his shirtsleeves within an inch of their lives. It's as if he graduated from bar-belling trees to tanks.

"What?" he snaps indignantly.

I shouldn't hang on his every word, but I do. Who's he talking to? Is someone complaining about me? Because I've been crushing it. Taking double shifts. All smiles. Amped up like an Energizer bunny. Nobody works as hard as I do, and not just for the tips. I have the Bishop legacy to maintain.

And yes, I may have mixed up an order here and there, or spilled one tiny little kid's milk. But I fixed every last mistake. And the *milk spill Boomerang clip* the kids posted got a ton of love on TikTok. Granted, the putrid dairy after-smell was wafting about for weeks, but thankfully, it's gone. Almost.

"No. No way," I hear Mark say, chuckling. I frown hard. I know that laugh. That's his evil laugh.

It's the laugh he had when he and Brian set a rope snare and trapped me in it, which, in my defense, I was eight. It was also the laugh that accompanied that nasty bowl of foul-tasting jellybeans and his insistence that girls couldn't eat them. He knew what he was doing. Throwing down a double-dog dare in the face of the female race. Well, I ate every last one. And whoever decided that vomit and boogers were palatable should be shot.

He also had that very same annoying laugh when he came up with that stupid nickname—

"Choir Girl?" he says with a scoff.

Fire fills my face as my grip on the door handle tightens.

This is the same man who tosses nicknames like *babe* or *princess* at every walking vagina in town, but for me, I'm simply Choir Girl. I mean, sure, I was in the church choir. And not just because everyone there was nice or that they handed out cocoa and cookies after every performance, which I lived for, but because Mom was there, too. It was our space as much as anyone else's.

"Me with Choir Girl?" He says it as if disgusted. By this point, I'm already inappropriately one foot in the office and charging straight at him. But Mark doesn't notice and just keeps going.

"Not with a ten-foot pole," he says with another scoff, and half of my heart shatters as he goes from being cold to cruel. "Make that a hundred-and-ten-foot pole. She's too"—he pauses for a moment for just the right word, the wheel in his mind landing on—"Jess."

Seriously? It's bad enough that he's banished me like a dwarf planet in my own brother's solar system. Why talk about me at all? Oh, that's right. Because he's Mark.

I bite my cheek, my face burning with more emotions than I can count. Frozen with indecision—to leave or to knee him in the groin—I blink away my stubborn tears just as he turns around. "Not even if the fate of mankind was dependent on my dick connecting with her vag—"

His mouth snaps shut, and I narrow my eyes.

He hangs up. For the longest second in history, I stare down the first man to make my *Vow to Hate for All Eternity* list. And that's not just my period talking.

"Jess," he says with a huff, annoyed. "Ever hear of knocking?" He walks over to his desk.

He did not just say that. *Ever hear of not talking shit behind someone's back, butt-munch?*

My mouth falls open, and I can feel every last one of my freckles catch fire. "Oh, I'm sorry, Your Royal Highness. Is that the proper etiquette? Knocking so I don't disturb you being an asshat?"

"Asshat?" His steps stop cold. He spins, facing me. "Well, this asshat happens to be your boss for today, Jess. That is, if you were working, which you shouldn't be. How about you come back tomorrow?"

Is that why Tyler told me to stay home? Because of Mark? When I could've used those tips? I feel my anger rise to a dangerous high as I stand my ground. "How about you give me an apology?"

When he rolls his eyes, I poke him in his dumb, stone-hard chest. *What am I doing?*

His eyes dart to my finger, then to my eyes. "I—" I take a breath, my chin defiant. "I deserve an apology," I snap.

He edges closer into my space. "Haven't you heard? In life, you never get what you deserve, Jess. Only what you can negotiate. Move it along, Choir Girl."

Again with the name? "Make me," I say in total stupid-brazen disregard for my stand-in boss. But I can't back down. Instead, I step up to him, toe-to-toe. I'm keenly aware of the childishness of my action considering the man has, oh, I don't know, a yard of height on me.

My stare-down is feeble, pathetic, really. I blame his eyes. They're gold now—charged and deadly—like some wild exotic cat I'm stupid enough to be in a staring contest with.

Two knocks chop at the door.

"Come in," he barks.

"Hey, hey, hey." Brian's voice is too familiar to both of us, but neither of us budges. My brother wraps a casual arm around me as if the death-glare crossfire isn't happening at all. He pulls me back and leans over to Mark. "I thought we had a talk about this."

I whip my head to Brian. "A talk about what?"

"Nothing." Mark's reply is quick. Too quick. He retreats behind his desk. *Coward*.

I turn my attention to Brian, breaking down his resolve with my angriest angry eyes. "What talk?"

He shrugs, his guilty smile on full display. "Nothing," he says, rushing me out of the room with both hands on my shoulders. "Mark and I need to chat, sis. See you later."

Before I get too far with a protest, the door slams in my face.

"*Argh*." I stomp my foot. I still need my check. Maybe if I'd taken Anita up on that lunch, I wouldn't be consumed with hangry rage. Between my hunger and my period, there's only one solution: full-blown annihilation. Crazed, I plow down the door, guns blazing.

"Why'd you hang up on me?" Brian asks Mark.

"What?" I glare down my enemies, Tweedle Dumb and

Tweedle Asshat, trying to make sense of why Mark's dick and my vag would ever come up in their conversation.

What the hell?

When Anita asked me about Mark, did I say, *"Me? With the dildo of the century? Not even if my vagina was on fire and his dick was the only way to put it out."* Wait, that came out wrong. And of course, I didn't. At least, not with my outside voice.

Instead of being a half-decent person, Mark clasps his hands and cocks his head in that arrogant way he always does. "Remember our little talk about knocking, Jess?"

It's as if his balls are begging to be kicked so hard, they lodge in that vacant space where his brain should be.

Fire licks at my good senses. I'm so ready to hand him that perfect ass of his on a platter, but the second I open my mouth, he adds, "I'd hate to see you lose your job for something as trivial as manners."

Stunned, I stare. *He'd really fire me over this?*

And what about Brian? Instead of standing up for me, my idiot big brother is just standing there. Like a big, dumb oaf, he's doing nothing but warning me with his eyes and a slow shake of his head.

Brian's right. I know he's right. He's leaving in a few days and taking this worthless sack of shit with him.

I should stay calm because I don't want this job, I need it. And not even for the money. Without it, I'm more or less alone. Rex is stationed in New Jersey. Close, but never close enough. And Cade is away in some god-forsaken part of the world that feels as unreachable as the moon.

Tears threaten fast. Too fast. As soon as he says, "Well, what do you know? Even choir girls have manners," no-holds-barred atomic anger wins.

I see the stack of checks on the desk, miraculously in alphabetical order. Mine's right on top. I snatch it up and stuff it in my pocket.

"Go to hell, Mark Donovan." And once again, when faced with the most beautiful man I've ever seen, my brain snaps in two, and I do the unthinkable. "I. Quit."

Pulse racing, I rush out of the room, determined not to cry like a girl or beg for my job. How did today end up like this?

I should've spent today planning the sendoff of the century for the brother of the year. Instead, I'm stuck spending the better part of it finding a new job and hating the both of them.

Asshat, one.

Choir Girl, zero.

CHAPTER 3
Mark

A FIST of fucking titanium flies from out of nowhere and slams me square in the chest. "Ow." My tone is pure *what the hell?*

It's true, I know better than to pick a fight with Jess. And I am technically the grown-up. Well, with her being eighteen and all, I guess she's a grown-up too. But I swear to God, that woman gets under my skin like lava-coated chiggers. Or maybe it's the guilt.

Brian and I know the price of his extended leave. It was a deal with the devil. Saying our next mission will be dangerous is like saying the Pope sometimes prays. There's a good chance we'll never see our families again, and the last thing I needed was to face off with Jess and her big, blue, soul-searching eyes. Hell, I can't even bear to look my mother in the eye.

Guns blazing, Brian lays into me. "You fire my sister five days before our next deployment?"

I didn't fire her. She quit. But with Brian glaring me down, there's no use arguing that technicality. Flustered, I point a finger at him. "This is your fault."

"My fault?"

"For giving me the fucking third degree and accusing me of making a play for Jess. Which she overheard. Thanks a fucking heap."

"Ah." He flicks a speck of dust from the desk. "How was I supposed to know you'd have that conversation with the door opened?"

I wave both arms in the air. "Now you know. And Jess was eavesdropping. *Again*. Her own bad habit brought this on."

Brian gives me a *don't fuck with the Bishops* face. "I can't have your back if things aren't square with Jess."

I rub at the ice pick driving into the base of my neck. "Well, technically, she quit."

When Brian hits me this time, he doesn't hold back. The man packs a punch like a battering ram. "Fix it, fucker."

I look at him as if a dick sprouted from the top of his head. "How? You know your sister. She's earned every last flaming strand of that red hair of hers. Fuck, we haven't spoken in years, and this is our reunion." I huff and lift my chin to the sky. "She hates me."

He shrugs. "Well, considering your first conversation in years is to threaten her job, her hating you seems validated."

"Is it my fault you made me say I wouldn't make moves on your sister with my outside voice?"

"Is it my fault you'll hump everything from a hydrant to a lamppost, and it wasn't exactly a stretch?"

I gesture at the door. "Clearly, you had nothing to worry

about." I adjust my pants from behind the desk. *Yeah, that's a bald-faced lie.*

"Clearly." Brian shakes his head. "You can't talk to her like she's twelve. She isn't."

Duh. One look at her ass told me that.

I remain stone-faced as Brian continues to lambast me. "You don't understand. Jess is stressed, too. With all the shit she's going through—" He clams up.

My ears perk up. "What's she going through?" I ask, tiptoeing as I pry.

He shakes it off. "Nothing. Just, *er*, woman stuff."

Enough said. The last thing I need to hear about is the world of Jess's uterus, though it does explain her flying off the fucking handle. With Jess, Moody is her middle name. Plus, with how full her breasts are and—

Where the fuck did that come from? I scramble to wipe the image from my mind. *Can we change the subject already?*

Brian drones on. "She's not a child anymore. And you're only filling in for the day, dickwad. Don't make me call your mommy on you."

"I know she's not a child."

While the very full-grown woman was busting my balls, it took every sheer ounce of willpower to avoid staring at those full, pouty lips. *Fuck*, she can't come back here. At least, not while I'm here. This is my funeral in the making.

Hmm. I think it through. Because I also can't *not* bring her back. Brian would murder me—*Saw* movie style.

I offer a solution. "She can consider herself on paid vacation until we leave. This way, the two of you can spend some time together."

And she'll be far the hell away from me.

Brian socks me again. Playfully, this time, but considering he gave it all he had the last round, I wince. "I guess you'd better find her and tell her that."

My eyes shoot wide. "You're her brother. Why don't you find her and tell her?"

"Because it's not my mess. It's yours. And we have our entire next mission to clean up after each other." He winks, the smartass, and heads for the door. "You know my baby sis would love to tend bar," he sings at me on his way out.

I throw a stress ball at his head. And miss.

He chuckles. "And they call you a sharpshooter," he calls out as he closes the door behind him.

Fucker.

I scroll through my phone until I find Jess's number, filed under "CG." I shoot her a text and wait her out.

Can we talk?

An hour later, after a thorough review of Zac's new inventory system, I check my phone. Still no response from Jess, so I try again.

I really need to talk to you.

By the time I've finished reviewing next month's menus with the staff, getting the seating arrangements for the Whitney wedding changed to accommodate nearly two hundred people instead of one hundred people, and reconciling the accounting for the month, my brain is fried.

I blow out a breath. Not a word from Choir Girl.

So, I do the unthinkable. I apologize.

Sorry I was an asshat. Please call back.

A text pings back, but the small surge of relief is instantly snuffed out. It isn't Jess. It's Brian. Even his text looks unhinged.

Did you talk to Jess???

Brian sends me a screenshot. Her phone finder app has her pinned on possibly the worst street in Albany. Without even speaking to him, I know Brian's about to lose his shit. Hell, my heart's beating out of my rib cage, and I'm half a breath away from losing my own shit.

What the fuck is she doing there?

Keep calm, I tell myself. If I'm panicked, Brian will panic tenfold.

I lock my voice into casual mode and call. "I've texted her several times. She hasn't returned my texts, but that's nothing new, considering her nickname for me is sometimes Satan. Have you tried calling her?"

"Yes, dumbass. Tried that first. I'm heading that way, but I'm home." The Bishop home is buried in a southwest pocket of Adirondack Park—at least an hour and a half from Albany. His voice rises, unnerved. "I need you to—"

"I'll take care of it. I'm leaving now."

I grab the nearest keys and rush out the front, nearly plowing down Anita. "Sorry, I'm in a hurry."

"Wait." She blocks my path. "Did Jess find you?"

"Yes," I grumble, irritated. Now I just need to find her.

"Oh, good. I know she was worried about getting that watch for Brian."

Impatient, I mutter, "What watch?" as I move around her and make my way to the truck.

Anita keeps pace, shoving her phone in my face. "This watch."

I check out the price tag. All her paychecks for two months wouldn't cover that watch. "How is she paying for a four-thousand-dollar watch?"

"She isn't. Some guy is selling his old one."

Of course. Because that's what people do. Sell four-thousand-dollar watches for a fraction of the price. It happens every day.

I get in the truck, slam the gas, punch the dashboard, and shout, "*Fuuuck!*"

Ready for more of Mark Donovan & Jess Bishop?
1-CLICK NOW>> MARKED

About the Author

Lexxi James is a USA Today bestselling author of romantic suspense. Her feats in multi-tasking include binge watching Netflix and sucking down a cappuccino in between feverish typing and loads of laundry.

She lives in Ohio with her teen daughter and the man of her dreams.

www.LexxiJames.com

Printed in Great Britain
by Amazon